EL LECTOR

ABOUT THE AUTHOR

William Durbin was born in Minneapolis and lives on Lake Vermilion, at the edge of the Boundary Waters Canoe Area Wilderness in northeastern Minnesota. He formerly taught English at a small rural high school and composition at a community college and has supervised writing research projects for the National Council of Teachers of English, the Bingham Trust for Charity, and Middlebury College. His wife, Barbara, is also a teacher, and they have two grown children.

William Durbin has published biographies of Tiger Woods and Arnold Palmer, as well as several books for young readers, among them *The Broken Blade, Wintering, Song of Sampo Lake*, and *Blackwater Ben. The Broken Blade* won the Great Lakes Book Award for Children's Books and the Minnesota Book Award for Young Adult Fiction.

Visit the author's Web site at williamdurbin.com.

EL LECTOR

William Durbin

Pineapple Press, Inc.
Sarasota, Florida

Inquiries should be addressed to:
Pineapple Press, Inc.
P.O. Box 3889
Sarasota, Florida 34230
www.pineapplepress.com

Library of Congress Cataloging-in-Publication Data

Durbin, William, 1951–
  El lector / William Durbin. — First edition.
      pages   cm
      Summary: "Thirteen-year-old Bella wants to be a lector just like her grandfather, who sits on a special platform in the cigar factory, reading great novels, the newspaper, and union news to workers as they roll the cigars. Being a lector is an important role in their immigrant community. But the hard times of the Depression mean that Bella must go to work in the factory; her hope of getting the education a lector needs seems impossible. Meanwhile, the factory workers and owners clash. People lose jobs, innocent workers are arrested, and the Ku Klux Klan prowls the area. And then there are those amazing new radios showing up all over town. Could the radio take the place of the lector? Bella must decide her own future and help her people preserve their history."—Provided by publisher.
      ISBN 978-1-56164-678-4 (pbk.)
      I. Title.
PZ7.D9323Le 2014
[Fic]—dc23

                                                                        2013031305

Cover design by Jennifer Borresen
Printed in the United States of America

EL LECTOR

To the citizens of Ybor City,
who believed in the power of stories
to enlighten and transform

CHAPTER 1
The Paradise Tree

The paradise tree above Bella Lorente's head was as wide as it was tall, spreading its green canopy over the roof of the El Paraíso cigar factory. Bella sat on the lawn below the open windows of the second-floor workroom and listened as her grandfather read to the workers who were rolling cigars. It was Saturday, and the March sun was warm. Grandfather's resonant voice carried out over the wind-rippled grass.

Behind the factory a dozen brightly colored kites flew over an open field. Bella heard her younger brother Pedro and his friends laughing as they unreeled their strings and steered their homemade kites higher. The larger kites, made out of red, green, and blue tissue paper, hung in perfect balance in the magical blue sky, their white tails swishing from side to side. The smaller kites, like Pedro's, made from plain brown paper, dipped and veered as they rode the gusty wind.

Bella turned her attention to Grandfather's reading. As El Paraíso's *lector*, Roberto García sat on an elevated platform in the main workroom for four hours each day and entertained two hundred cigar rollers by reading news, literature, and politics. One of Ybor City's most respected *lectores*, Grandfather always wore a white suit coat, a white shirt with gold cuff links, a silk tie, and dark pants.

Grandfather's performances were so popular that women from the neighborhood, many with babies in their arms, walked to the factory at midday and spread their blankets on the lawn to listen. Today, Bella and two dozen women sat quietly, their faces marked by leaf shadows and their eyes intent on the story of *Don Quixote de La Mancha.*

"What a gift Señor García has," a young mother whispered to Bella. "It's not so much what he says as how he says it. So many *lectores* use microphones these days, but feel the *fuerza de grito*—the strength of his voice! Every reading is like music."

Bella smiled. She'd heard Grandfather read the story of Quixote's quest before, but she never tired of the funny, sad tale. Grandfather was reading the famous passage where Quixote charges a windmill. Mistaking the blades for the arms of a giant, the nearsighted knight lowers his lance and spurs his horse forward. Grandfather's voice mirrored the pounding of the hooves, the creaking of the windmill arms; and Bella heard the cigar workers chuckle as the knight toppled from his saddle.

When Grandfather closed his book there was a moment of silence. Then one worker slapped his *chaveta*, his rounded cigar knife, on the wooden workbench. Soon two hundred blades were clapping down in appreciation and filling the factory hall with a dull thunder.

Bella left the picnic basket she'd prepared for Grandfather under the tree and hurried upstairs to the workroom. Grandfather stood and bowed to the cigar makers. A shock of silver hair fell onto his forehead, and the ends of his salt-and-pepper mustache turned up in the hint of a smile. When the noise of the *chavetas* faded and the workers pushed back their chairs for the lunch break, Grandfather put on his Panama hat and stepped down from his oak lectern.

"Good afternoon, Bella." Grandfather beamed. "Welcome to paradise."

"Calling this factory *El Paraíso* doesn't make it paradise." Bella wrinkled her nose at the clouds of blue cigar smoke that filled the hall.

"So the smell of damp tobacco and cigars is not your idea of heaven?" Grandfather said.

A cigar maker tipped his hat to Grandfather as he walked past. "A fine reading, Señor García," he said. The rollers were skilled craftsmen who regarded Grandfather as a fellow artist.

"*Gracias.*" Grandfather nodded to the man.

Bella waved the smoke from her face. "I'm glad you don't smoke." Most workers smoked at their benches and took three cigars home each evening, but Grandfather never used tobacco.

"I need to protect my voice. But don't forget that cigar money fills your soup pot at home."

"Mama's job is doing laundry."

"And where do you suppose her customers dirty their clothes?" Grandfather motioned toward the rows of benches, their tops stained dark from tobacco leaves. Then he offered his arm to Bella. "Shall we dine on the lawn today, señorita?"

As they stepped outside, Grandfather looked up at the clusters of tiny yellow blossoms on the paradise tree. "Now will you admit that we have entered paradise?"

"The flowers are beautiful," Bella said, admiring the delicate petals that swayed in the breeze and gave off a sweet perfume. Bella had played under the paradise tree from the time she was a little girl. Its broad crown of waxy, pink-veined leaves shaded the lawn and the factory windows in deep green.

Bella spread out a blanket while Grandfather held the picnic basket. "What treats do we have today?" He lifted a corner of the white cloth.

"Cold soup," Bella said, "and fresh bread from Ferlita's."

"You made *gazpacho Andaluz!*" Grandfather smiled as he sat down. "A feast fit for the gods."

Bella didn't care for the Spanish tomato soup, but it was Grandfather's favorite lunch. Though Bella was only thirteen, she'd been helping Mama with the housework and doing her part in caring for the four younger children since she was eleven. That was the year her papa, Domingo, had been killed on a tobacco-buying trip in Cuba. He and Grandfather had planned to start a cigar factory called García & Lorente. Papa had their life savings with him on the day he was robbed and murdered.

Grandfather broke off a piece of bread and sniffed the

crust. Then he tasted the soup. *"¡Delicioso!"* He touched his napkin to his lips. "This soup would make Pijuan jealous."

Bella smiled. Pijuan was the head chef at the Columbia, the finest restaurant in Ybor. Since Grandfather didn't cook, he often ate there.

"What's in the newspapers today?" she asked. Grandfather subscribed to *La Gaceta* and *La Traduccion,* as well as two English papers, which he translated into Spanish and read to the workers.

"The usual trouble. Riots in Madrid. Martial law declared in Lima. But local matters worry me most."

"You mean the Tobacco Workers International Union vote?"

"Yes," Grandfather said. "If the TWIU wins, the Anglo business owners are threatening to form a citizens' committee. That would give a free hand to the vigilantes who want to crush the cigar makers' union. And you know, the Ku Klux Klan will keep attacking the union and the Negroes."

"Could it get as bad as last year?"

"Let's hope not."

Bella shuddered. Last year Anglo businessmen had backed a Klan mob that kidnapped a poor immigrant named John Hodaz from the police. After lynching him, they'd shot his body to pieces.

"Enough dark talk." Grandfather touched Bella's hand. "Let's enjoy this fine meal." He tore off another piece of bread and dipped it into his soup. "I was just thinking how you look more like your grandmother every day."

"Oh, Grandfather."

"It's true. I'll never forget the day an artist asked my Belicia

5

to sit for the portrait they still use on El Paraíso's most famous label, the Paraíso Perfecto. The painter saw us in a sidewalk café. He walked up to Belicia and bowed, saying, 'In all of my travels I have not witnessed such beauty.' "

"Was she shy?" Bella thought of the painting in Grandfather's parlor that showed Bella's namesake, Belicia García, in a sleeveless white gown. Her dark brown eyes sparkled, and she wore a single red rose in her shiny black hair. Bella had admired the portrait from the time she was little and tried to imagine what her grandmother had been like.

"She was modest," Grandfather said, "and tall and graceful like you."

"But my hair and my eyes are so plain compared to hers." Bella touched the tight braids that her mother had plaited.

"I tell you, when the light shines a certain way—" Grandfather stopped at a shout from the field. "Could that be Pedro?"

"I'd better check." Bella set down her napkin and jogged past the loading dock to the field. One little boy was crying and pointing at Pedro.

Bella walked up. "What happened now?"

"That boy lost his kite, and he's blaming me." Pedro curled his lower lip in a pout.

"You cut the string." The boy's voice trembled.

"It's not my fault," Pedro mumbled. He held his kite in one hand and a stick wound with string in the other.

Bella saw a glint of metal on his kite tail. She bent down and lifted it. On a matchstick spliced between the last two knots, Pedro had taped a pair of razor blades that would cut any kite string they crossed. "How many times has Mama warned you about kite fighting?" Bella asked. "Someone could get hurt with those blades whipping through the air."

"All the fellows are doing it." Pedro kept his voice low and looked out of the corner of his eye to see if his friends were watching.

"That doesn't make it right," she said. "You're eleven years old! You know better." Pedro stared at the ground and wiped a dirty fist across his wet cheek.

"So how can we make things right, Pedro?"

"What do you mean?" He peered up at her. Pedro was short for his age and so skinny that his pants looked two sizes too big.

"Shouldn't we do something about this boy losing his kite?" If only Papa were alive to help discipline Pedro. As difficult as Papa's death had been for the rest of the family, the loss had been even harder on Pedro.

Pedro glanced at the boy. Finally he said, "I suppose I could give him my kite."

"That would be the honorable thing to do." Grandfather's deep voice startled them. They hadn't heard him approach. "And honor is the only currency of value in this life."

Bella smiled. That was one of Grandfather's favorite expressions.

"I'd better take these off first," Pedro said, untying the razor blades from the tail and handing the kite to the boy.

"A wise decision," Grandfather said.

"Try using your head next time," Bella said, wrapping the razor blades in her handkerchief and slipping them into her skirt pocket.

"Thank you for the fine meal, Bella." Grandfather handed her the basket and folded blanket. "Now, back to my reading."

CHAPTER 2
Goat de La Mancha

By the time Bella and Pedro walked past the factory, Juan Fernandez, the *presidente de la lectura*, was ringing a bell in the second-story hall to quiet the workers so Grandfather could begin. Juan headed a workers' committee that hired the *lector*. The same committee helped select the political essays and union newsletters that Grandfather read, but the cigar rollers voted on the novels. Though most of the workers couldn't read, they believed in the power of knowledge and paid Grandfather's salary out of their own pockets.

Many of Ybor City's *lectores* read novels right after lunch, but Grandfather preferred to use the lazy *siesta* hour for reading labor news. That left the factory lawn empty of listeners until Grandfather's final session of the day, when he performed poetry, short stories, and excerpts from plays and operas.

Bella paused at the edge of the sidewalk. "Listen to how far his voice carries," she told Pedro. She had always dreamed of being *el lector*, just like Grandfather. When she was little she'd stood in her parlor and pretended she was at a tall lectern as she read storybooks and poems to her family. When she finished, Papa called, *"Viva, Bella!"* and clapped his hands on the table.

Today Grandfather's pure Castilian Spanish was as clear as if he was standing right beside them: "Before I read a Bakunin essay, which explains how the wealthy use property to enslave the working man, I have news about our comrades in the coalfields of Harlan, Kentucky. The miners who were recently fired for joining the union have been evicted from their homes. At this very hour many women and children lack basic necessities. On Friday we'll be taking up a collection for them."

"Who cares about coal miners?" Pedro asked. "There's still a good wind." He looked over the roof at the kite tails waggling in the sky. "If you want to listen, I can go back and play."

"No," Bella said, "Mama needs you this afternoon." Washing clothes was the only work Mama could manage and still keep an eye on her children. Grandfather often tried to hire help for Mama or give her money, but she always said, *"Merced recibida, libertad vendida"*—who receives a gift, sells his liberty. Mama made an exception in allowing Grandfather to pay their rent.

As Bella and Pedro walked down Twentieth Street toward home, Bella said, "Smell the ocean." Hillsborough Bay lay several miles south of Ybor City, but an ocean breeze often carried the scents of sea salt and mudflats and mangroves into town.

Just then a panpipe trilled, followed by a singsong voice: *"Con dinero, o sin dinero."*

"The *pirulí* man!" Pedro said.

A man in a butcher's apron and straw hat came around the corner carrying a banana stalk stuck full of cone-shaped lollipops. His call of "With money or without money" meant that he would take either a penny or a coupon as payment.

"Could we—" Pedro began.

"After what happened with your kite?"

Pedro trudged beside Bella. Chatter in Spanish and Italian came from the shops, and a wagon heaped with sacks of coffee beans rattled down the cobbled street.

Pedro came back to life when they turned onto Ninth Avenue and caught the scent of fresh bread from Ferlita's Bakery. "I'm hungry."

"I'll fix you something," Bella said. It was hard not to think of food all the time, living just down the street from Ferlita's giant brick-domed ovens, which stayed on twenty-four hours a day.

Their neighborhood of one-story *casitas* was full of Spanish, Cuban, and Italian families who worked in the cigar factories. Half a block from home, Bella and Pedro heard, "Baa huh huh!"

"How does she know we're coming?" Pedro asked.

"I've tried tiptoeing up the street, but she always hears me," Bella said as they walked around the back of their white *casita*.

Their little goat, Rocinante, was tethered to a broad oak in the backyard. She trotted toward them, her stubby tail sticking up and head bobbing. "Such a pretty girl," Bella said as the goat lifted her chin to have her neck scratched. Rocinante was so vain that she pranced in a half circle when anyone told her she was pretty. She had little nubs of ears and soft black fur that shone in the afternoon sun, and she loved it when Bella scratched her tufted beard and her toes.

Lots of people in Ybor City kept animals. Bella's neighbors raised chickens, rabbits, and pigeons.

Mama stepped out onto the back porch. "I'm glad you're home. The baby's been—" She eyed Pedro. "Where's your kite?"

"Ahh—" Pedro faltered. "I—"

"Have you been getting into mischief again?" Mama said. "I swear I'll hang myself from the clothesline if you shame this family one more time."

"Kites have a way of flying away, don't they?" Bella said, wondering why she bothered to stick up for Pedro when he'd been so mean.

He nodded eagerly.

"And all morning you begged me to cut up that sheet for your kite tail." Mama pushed her kerchief back with her fingers. Her eyes looked tired. She was wearing a long black dress and an apron. Though Papa had died two years ago, she still dressed in mourning clothes.

Bella carried the picnic basket through the door.

"Would you watch Julio?" Mama asked. "Pedro can help me carry in the laundry so we can start ironing."

"May I slice some bread for Pedro first?" Bella poured

water into the blue porcelain basin beside the sink and washed her hands.

Pedro opened the icebox and poured himself a glass of milk. "Wash your hands, too," Bella said.

Pedro sat at the table and ate while Bella bounced Julio on her knee. Julio once had bad stomachaches, and the doctor advised feeding him goat's milk. The milk helped, so Grandfather bought Rocinante.

"If a man must own a goat," Grandfather said when he led her into their yard, "it should be a proper Spanish breed."

"Why doesn't it have ears?" Pedro had asked.

"It's a La Mancha—no ordinary goat, mind you, but one that's descended from the ancient herds of Cordova, Spain."

"Are you making that up?" Bella laughed. "*La Mancha,* as in *Don Quixote?*"

"On my honor."

Now, when Pedro started out the back door, Bella said, "Make sure you hang up the washtub and scrub board for Mama."

Pedro nodded. A washtub for rinsing the clothes hung against the back wall of the house, along with a stirring stick, scrub board, and hand wringer. Another tub stayed propped up on bricks in the backyard. Once the clothes were boiled and rinsed, Mama hung them on a line strung between a tall magnolia and two live oaks. A tin bathtub also hung from a nail on the back wall. For Saturday baths the tub was set behind a lattice screen on the back porch.

Bella turned to Julio, who was sitting on the floor. "Is it

time for our walk?" Bella helped him up. Julio had been born four months after Papa's death. Bella was proud that Julio's dark, curly hair and his square chin told the world he was Domingo Lorente's son, but she was sad because he always reminded her that Papa was gone. Her papa had been taken away when he was so young!

Julio wobbled up and down the hallway. Like other *casitas*, their house was tall and narrow. It had been built in shotgun style: a long hall on the left side of the house ran from the front parlor past the two bedrooms to the kitchen. All the rooms were small and paneled with dark pine beadboard. Twelve-foot ceilings and tall windows helped circulate the air during the hot summers.

Clutching Bella's hand, Julio turned into the bedroom that Bella shared with her younger sisters, Isabel and Juanita.

Julio aimed a finger at the window and said, "What's that?" When Bella said, *"La ventana,"* Julio repeated it. Bella said, "Window," so he could learn the English along with the Spanish and have a head start when he entered school.

He pointed to the iron bed.

"La cama," Bella answered, and as he traced an embroidered butterfly on her quilt, she whispered, *"la mariposa."*

Julio wobbled back to the hall and turned into the front bedroom. He walked past Pedro's bed and his crib to the far wall and touched a tooled leather belt that hung from a bright silver buckle. *"Padre?"*

"Padre." Bella nodded. The belt was the one legacy that Domingo had left to his family. Hidden in the lining was a tiny pouch of rare tobacco seeds that Domingo had purchased in

Havana just before his murder. No matter how difficult things got, Mama felt better knowing the seeds were there. In an emergency the seeds could be sold, or perhaps one day the Lorentes would use them to start the cigar business that had been Domingo's dream.

When Julio stepped into the parlor, Bella clapped her hands. "You're walking like a big boy!"

"Big boy." Julio pulled her onto the front porch. Heat waves rose from the paving bricks in the street, and the sun-bleached *casitas* across the street floated in golden light. Over the shouts of boys playing stickball, *el riquiti,* Bella heard the distant clang of the trolley downtown.

The bell in the clock tower at the Regensburg Factory tolled two o'clock. *"El reloj."* Bella used the Spanish word for *clock,* the local name for the factory.

"El reloj," Julio repeated as the bronze echo rolled over their heads and out toward the invisible sea.

Bella thought of how Papa used to walk her up the street to the Regensburg's redbrick tower just before noon. They'd stand hand in hand, waiting for the tolling to begin. As the huge bell boomed, Papa would kneel and whisper, *"El reloj."*

CHAPTER 3
La Séptima

Juanita and Isabel ran in from playing. "Will you tell us Grandfather's story?" Juanita asked Bella. She was short and curly-haired like Pedro, and she had a little dimple on her chin. She never stopped talking.

"After dinner," Bella said.

"Did he read Don Quixote again?" Isabel asked. Her green eyes were dreamy. She was tall and slender like Grandfather and Bella, and she always thought before she spoke.

"Oh, yes," Bella said. "Help me put the rice on the table."

Each evening after supper Bella retold the part of the novel Grandfather had performed that day. Bella read the chapters on her own to keep up with the story. If she studied hard and trained her voice, she hoped to entertain a hall filled with cigar workers one day. Just like *El Lector.*

Tonight, even Pedro helped clear the dishes so Bella could begin. "What's happened so far?" she asked.

Juanita told about Don Quixote's quest, his loyal friend Sancho Panza, and his knighthood.

"Don't forget that he wore a helmet and a buckler," Pedro said. "And he carried a big sword and a lance."

Bella tried to tell the story at the same pace as Grandfather, taking her time to picture the field, the giant windmills, and Sancho's warning to Quixote. Then came the charge. . . .

Just as Bella finished, a voice hollered from the back porch. "Where's my girl? It's time for our Saturday-night promenade! Seventh Avenue awaits."

"Tía Lola!" Isabel and Juanita cheered as their aunt walked through the back door. Mama didn't care about fashion, but Tía Lola's short hair was dyed red blond and her eyebrows were pencil thin.

Pedro jumped up. "Did you visit the *pirulí* man, Tía Lola?"

"It so happens that I met such a man on my way here, and"—she reached into the pocket of her bright yellow dress— "he sold me these." She handed a lollipop to each of the children, who clapped and thanked her.

"So how are things going with Fernando?" Mama asked.

"I'm too young to settle down," Lola said.

"You're thirty-one years old."

"Marriage would cut down on the number of boyfriends I

could have." Lola winked at Bella. "Besides, Fernando expects me to become a housewife, and I'm not about to give up my job." Aunt Lola was a master cigar maker at the Rafael Fuente Factory, where she specialized in filling custom orders for rich American businessmen and European royalty.

"So why aren't you dressed up?" Aunt Lola turned to Bella.

"I was going to wear this."

"Jeepers creepers, do we have to go through this again?" Lola said. "We're not visiting a nunnery." Lola rolled up the waistband of Bella's calf-length skirt until the hem hung just below her knee. "Perfect," she said. "The easiest way to interest young men is to raise the hem a few inches."

"That's the sort of interest Bella can do without." Mama frowned.

"You've got to let her grow up, Rosa. When I was her age I had to beat the boys off with a stick." Lola grinned at Bella. "And a haircut would do wonders for you." She fingered Bella's black braids.

"I admire Bella's modesty," Mama said. Bella had wanted to cut her hair for a year, but Mama said braids were more proper for a young girl.

Lola studied Bella. "Stand up straight and be proud of your figure." She tried to unfold Bella's arms from her chest. "Lord knows, gravity takes over soon enough."

"Lola García!" Mama said.

Just then someone in the backyard yelled, "Would you stop it!"

"That must be Mary," Bella said.

"Rocinante's trying to get her purse again," Isabel said.

"We're in the kitchen," Bella called.

"That goat will chew on anything," Lola said. "She's got some hot Cuban blood in her veins."

"Grandfather says Rocinante is pure Spanish," Isabel said.

"Your grandfather worries too much about purity," Lola said.

"Hi, Mary." Bella hugged her friend. Like Bella, Mary was shy about her height. She had frizzy black hair that she parted on the side, and her smooth skin was a shade darker than Bella's. Mary's face was always set in a quiet smile.

"We'll have to work on your wardrobe some other time. For now"—Lola took Bella by the shoulders and turned her around—"we'll brighten you up." She pulled a tube of lipstick out of her purse and did a quick paint job on Bella's lips.

"Me too." Juanita thrust her face forward.

When Lola finished with Juanita, she offered the lipstick to Isabel and Mary, but they shook their heads.

Bella knew that Mary's mother forbade her to use makeup. Mary was the real reason Bella wanted to wear a plain skirt tonight. Thanks to gifts from Lola and Grandfather, Bella owned four different outfits, but Mary's only dress was threadbare and patched. Like most folks in Ybor, Mary's family had been struggling to survive the Depression. Her mother worked as a cleaning lady, and her father, who was a carpenter, had been forced to travel north looking for work.

Lola put her lipstick back in her purse. "Let's fix that collar for you." She turned down the collar of Mary's dress and smoothed her hair.

"Thanks," Mary said.

"My pleasure, honey," Lola said. "You're so pretty." Then she turned to Mama. "What time do you want these ladies home?"

"Eleven at the latest," Mama said.

"The dancing doesn't even start until eleven in Ybor." Lola did a half twirl and curtsied to Mary as Juanita and Isabel laughed.

"But you're only taking them to the movies. And remember, *you're* the chaperone." Mama turned to Bella. "Make sure your aunt behaves."

Bella chuckled. In Ybor City, mothers or aunts accompanied young girls when they went out in the evening, but Mama often joked that Lola was the one who needed the chaperoning.

"Do you want me to be like Mrs. Cianni?" Lola asked.

"Who?" Mary asked.

"Our neighbor," Bella said. "She's so strict that when her daughter went out on a date last summer with a boy who owned a car, she rode in the front seat while her daughter sat alone in the back."

"Sounds like my mom," Mary said.

"Let's get a wiggle on, or all the good seats in that petting pantry will be taken," Lola said.

"Would you stop!" Mama threw up her hands.

"Have a good evening, Rosa." Lola waved as they stepped outside.

"Bye, Mama," Bella called. She felt bad that Mama stayed home all the time. When Bella was a little girl, the high point of her week had been walking downtown to shop with Mama on Saturday, then watching her get ready to go out on a stroll with

Papa. But since Papa's funeral Mama hadn't ventured farther from home than Cannella's Market around the corner.

Lola grabbed Bella's and Mary's hands and swung their arms high. "La Séptima, here we come."

La Séptima was Seventh Avenue. On Saturday nights hundreds of people gathered at the clubs, movie houses, bars, and cafés. Cigar workers were known for spending all their money on payday. "Live as if you'll die tomorrow" was Aunt Lola's favorite saying.

At the end of the block a tall policeman smiled and tipped his cap. "Good evening, Miss García."

"Hi there, Billy," Lola said. Billy Burns was the most popular policeman in Ybor City.

"Have a pleasant time tonight, ladies."

As Burns whistled on his away, Lola said, "I just love the way a man looks in a well-pressed uniform."

"He'd almost be cute if he wasn't so old," Bella said.

"Old!" Lola said. "Billy's younger than I am!"

Bella and Mary giggled.

The sidewalks were overflowing. Vendors sang of tropical fruit, fresh-cut flowers, vegetables, and deviled crabs. The *manisero* man sold peanuts, the *heladero* man sherbet. The aroma of roasted coffee, hot bread, and cigars mingled with the spices of Italian and Cuban cooking. Groups of young men in their best white shirts and pants whistled and waved to each other, while young girls paraded in their fanciest dresses.

"Shall we promenade one time?" Lola asked.

Mary shook her head. "Not tonight, Tía Lola," Bella said.

Most young people walked a regular Saturday-night route, starting at Fourteenth Street. But Bella knew that Mary didn't want to walk down the main street. Not only was Mary's dress patched, but she was ashamed of her bright yellow shoes, which her mother had found in a sale bin the past fall. Mean boys called her Canary.

"You're a couple of killjoys," Lola said.

"We came to see a movie," Bella said.

"Clark Gable is handsomer than these skinny boys." Lola raised her voice to be heard over the crowd. "They look like starved chickens! But if I could get my hands on that Al Lopez—have either of you seen him tonight, by chance?—I'd marry that man in a minute." Lopez was a catcher who had been called up to Brooklyn a few years before. He was Ybor City's most famous citizen and its most eligible bachelor.

"He has a girlfriend," Mary said.

"Don't break my heart!"

"Besides, he's way too young for you," Bella laughed.

"Watch your tongue, vixen."

As they walked home from the movie, Bella asked, "Weren't Clark Gable and Greta Garbo a perfect couple?"

"I love a tall man with a mustache," Lola said. "Don't you, Mary?"

When Mary didn't answer, Bella said, "What's going on with you tonight?"

"What did you say?"

Bella stopped and looked at her. "Tell me what's wrong."

Tears welled up in Mary's eyes.

"What is it?" Bella said.

Mary dabbed her eyes with her sleeve. "My mother—"

"Are her lungs worse?" Bella asked. Mary's mother was recovering from a mild case of tuberculosis.

"She's fine," Mary said. "But you know things haven't been easy."

Bella nodded. Mary's father had lost his job the year before, so he'd gone to Philadelphia and worked in construction. After sending money to the family through the summer, he'd been laid off and headed west.

"It's been five months since we've heard from my dad." Mary looked down at the sidewalk. "Our rent is past due. . . . I'm afraid we might have to move to my grandma's."

"Not the one in Jacksonville?" Bella asked.

"Yes." Mary began to cry.

Bella reached into her skirt pocket to get a handkerchief. "Ouch." She jerked her hand back. Under the iron streetlamp she could see blood oozing from a thin slit on her fingertip.

"How'd you do that?" Mary blinked back her tears.

"I took some razor blades from Pedro this afternoon, and I forgot they were still in my pocket," Bella said.

"You yelped like a lobster pinched you." Lola laughed. "It's only a little cut." She pulled out a handkerchief and wrapped up the finger.

"Serves me right for being so forgetful." Bella tried to laugh, but the thought of losing Mary cut deeper than any blade.

CHAPTER 4
Sunday Dinner

When Bella woke the next morning, she tried to guess the direction of the wind before she opened her eyes. Today it wasn't the usual easterly breeze that brought the smell of bread down the street from Ferlita's Bakery. Nor was it a southerly wind carrying the sea scents from the bay, or a north wind bringing the odor of damp tobacco from El Paraíso. Instead, the sweet, tropical smell told her the breeze was drifting into town from the guava-processing plant to the west.

The first things Bella saw when she opened her eyes were two photographs hanging on her bedroom wall. One was a picture of the famous pilot Amelia Earhart, standing in front of her plane. The other was a present from Aunt Lola. It showed Luisa

Capetillo, an old friend of Lola's who had risen to the position of *lector*. Dressed in a man's white suit, hat, shirt, and tie, *La Lectura* posed proudly beside her reading platform. On the bottom of the photo she'd written: "To Lola, my *compadre.*"

Each morning Luisa's confident look inspired Bella to picture herself at a lectern. But Bella had shared her dream only with Mary and Lola.

"Laundry time." Mama spoke softly and touched Bella's shoulder so she wouldn't wake Juanita and Isabel.

"Why can't we rest on Sunday like normal people?" Bella groaned. Mama's clothes already smelled of woodsmoke and soap.

"Normal people don't do other folks' washing all week." Mama kept her voice low. "That leaves Sunday for our laundry."

Bella sighed as she got up and dressed. It wasn't fair that she had to climb out of bed when her neighbor Mr. Navarro was snoring next door. Since the *casitas* on their block were only a few feet apart and everyone left their windows open, there were no secrets in the neighborhood. In the evenings the porches worked like a telegraph system, spreading news from house to house. When Pedro and his friends got into trouble, their parents found out about it before the boys arrived home.

As Bella walked down the hallway, she heard Mama visiting with Mrs. Navarro. They often talked through their windows as they cooked or did the dishes.

Bella looked at her finger. The thin cut reminded her of Mary. If only Mary's father would write!

"Let's get moving." Mama stepped onto the back porch.

Not only did Bella help wash clothes on Sunday, but she and her sisters also had to clean the house, wash the windows, sweep the walk, and prepare for the family dinner with Grandfather and Aunt Lola. Though Pedro helped outside, Mama excused him from housework because he was a boy.

Bella knew she was lucky to have her grandfather visit so often. Most men in Ybor spent their free time in the local clubs and cafés, playing dominoes and drinking coffee, but Grandfather enjoyed being with his family. Though Mama was too proud to ask for help, Grandfather always bought food, and presents for the children. When Bella heard talk about how the Depression had hit Florida sooner and harder than the rest of America because of the real estate crash, she was especially grateful to Grandfather for watching over them.

The steeply angled rays of the sun flooded the backyard with green-gold light. As Bella stepped off the porch, a tiny, emerald-colored lizard darted behind their purple hibiscus. A fire crackled under the laundry tub where Mama stirred the clothes in the steaming water.

"It feels like summer already," Bella said, looking up into the pale tendrils of Spanish moss that trailed from the oak limbs. Just then the bell at Our Lady of Mercy tolled, calling the parishioners to early mass. Only a handful of people in their neighborhood attended church regularly.

After waiting for the sound to die away, Mama said, "The magnolia will be in full bloom soon."

Each spring Bella looked forward to seeing the giant white blossoms. The flowers were a foot across, and they had brilliant red seed cones that opened in autumn.

"Where's Rocinante?" Bella asked.

Mama looked up. "I hope she hasn't chewed through her rope and wandered off again."

"The rope's right here." Bella picked up a loop and gave it a tug. She heard a sad *Baa huh huh* coming from behind the oak. "Time for breakfast." Bella pulled harder on the rope, but the goat wouldn't budge.

"She must not be hungry," Mama said.

"Rocinante's always hungry." Bella followed the rope to the tree and peeked around it. "Hi there, pretty—" Bella stopped. "Oh my!"

"What's the matter?"

"Look at poor Rocinante," Bella said. The fur was half gone from the top of her head, and little patches of pink skin showed down her back. "That's all right, girl," Bella said. She knelt down to scratch the goat's chin whiskers.

"Who on God's green earth could have—" Mama turned toward the house. "Pedro!"

"What will that spoiled brat do next?" Bella asked.

Mama rousted Pedro out of bed and pulled him into the kitchen. "What did you do to that poor goat?"

"Does she look bad?" Pedro rubbed the sleep out of his eyes. "It was getting dark, and we couldn't see so good."

"We?"

"Joe and I. We watched the barber shave Grandfather the other morning, and we wanted to give it a try. Since neither of us have beards—"

"Thank heavens for small favors." Mama rolled her eyes. "You would have cut each other's throats."

"We figured Rocinante wouldn't mind if we practiced on her."

"That poor creature may never be the same!" Mama threw her hands skyward. "I swear I should hang myself from the clothesline and end all my miseries! You're not leaving the house for a week."

"But I didn't hurt nobody."

Mama cuffed Pedro on the shoulder as he scooted by. She dabbed her eyes with her handkerchief and whispered, "If only my Domingo, may his soul rest in peace, were here to set that boy straight."

By the time Bella and the girls had hung out the last load of laundry, the sun was blazing. "It's lucky we got an early start," Bella said.

"Do you want me to do goat duty?" Juanita asked. They had to make sure Rocinante didn't get loose and chew up the laundry.

"Poor Rocinante is too embarrassed to come out from behind that tree today," Isabel said.

As soon as the girls stepped into the kitchen, Mama handed Bella a paring knife. "Start chopping the peppers and onions for dinner."

"Is Pedro still in the parlor?" Juanita asked.

"A morning in the corner will encourage him to think before he starts shaving things," Mama said.

"He deserves it," Isabel said. "You'd think he'd have learned after snipping off his eyebrows last summer."

Lola was the first to arrive for Sunday dinner. "How about some help out here?" she yelled from the front porch. "My arms are breaking."

The children ran to the door. "Hooray!" Pedro said. "Tía Lola's brought a flan." Lola's caramel and egg custard was the children's favorite.

Pedro reached up for the plate. Lola held a bouquet of black-eyed Susans in her other hand.

"Not so fast." Lola lifted the plate high. "I expect a proper greeting."

"Good afternoon, Tía Lola." Pedro stretched on tiptoes to kiss her cheek. Then he took the dessert to the kitchen.

"For you, Rosa." Lola handed Mama the flowers.

"And how are my favorite girls?"

"Fine, Tía Lola," Isabel said.

Lola put her hand on Bella's shoulder. "Is Mary holding up?"

"She's doing the best she can," Bella said.

"I guarantee there'll be greater heartbreaks ahead for you both," Lola said.

"What a way to cheer me up!"

Lola stepped back and looked Bella up and down. "One thing that would improve your mood is standing up straighter. Remember what I've told you about posture? Lift your chin. Be proud of yourself." Juanita threw her shoulders back and stood at attention. "And why do you insist on wearing such baggy blouses?" Lola tugged at Bella's neckline, making her blush. "A little concealment can be a good strategy, but don't throw a tent over the whole camp."

"Would you stop that!" Mama called from the kitchen.

"Just trying to be helpful," Lola said.

"I hope I haven't missed dinner." A deep voice rumbled from the doorway. Grandfather carried a package wrapped in butcher paper.

"We can't eat until you come, Grandfather," Isabel said.

"And why is that?" Grandfather knelt down and looked into Isabel's green eyes.

"Because you bring the dinner!"

"So I do." He chuckled and handed the package to Mama as he rose. "Red snapper. Sebastiano selected the fillets specially for you." Sebastiano was one of Grandfather's oldest friends, and he ran a famous fish market in the city.

"So expensive," Mama said.

"My family deserves the best," Grandfather said. "Besides"— he hung his hat on a hook—"I had my share of tough times when we first came to Ybor City, and I promised myself that once I made my mark in the world I'd never do without."

"Did you go hungry when you were little?" Juanita asked.

"We always had food, even if it was only stale bread and beans. But the worst thing around here was the mud and the thick clouds of mosquitoes. Back then Ybor was surrounded by swamps. The snakes and alligators outnumbered the *tabaqueros*. Our drinking water was so muddy that we had to strain it with a rag." Isabel shivered. "Fellows joked that the water was too thick to drink but too thin to plow."

"Hard times may be returning," Aunt Lola said as Grandfather took a seat in the parlor.

"Are they cutting wages again?" Grandfather asked.

"I've heard we might lose another day."

"You'll lose more than that if the owners keep installing cigar-rolling machines," Grandfather said.

"They could never replace these." Lola held out her hands to Bella. "Are they not things of art?"

"Is that a new color?" Bella asked, studying Lola's red nails and her three gold rings.

"It's Paris Mist," Lola said.

"You have the hands of a concert pianist," Bella said.

"That's my girl." Lola patted Bella's arm.

"Machines or not, things are going to get a lot worse if the tobacco workers vote to strike again," Grandfather said.

"That might be our only hope," Lola said.

"Compromise is always the best policy."

"We can't keep flapping our gums and taking the cutbacks without a fight—"

"Lola," Mama interrupted, "would you mind helping me start the fish?"

"Of course." Lola followed Mama to the kitchen. Bella was grateful that Mama had stopped the union talk. Lola and Grandfather always argued when it came to labor matters. Though Grandfather read labor newsletters to the workers at El Paraíso, he believed the union leaders were too bold at times.

Juanita sat on Grandfather's knee. "If there were so many snakes and mosquitoes in the pioneer days, why did you come here?"

"Yes," Pedro said, "weren't things better in Asturias?"

Grandfather smiled. "We left Spain because my father was

tired of being lorded over by kings and churchmen. We came to the New World by way of Havana, where my father was hired as a *lector*. Later, we followed the cigar makers to Key West."

"And then the railroad came to Ybor," Isabel said.

"You've listened well to my stories." Grandfather chuckled. "Once Henry Plant brought his railroad and steamship lines to Tampa, Vicente Martinez Ybor started a cigar factory. Mr. Ybor invited me to move here with my beautiful Belicia and seek our fortune."

Grandfather paused. Bella had heard the rest of the story many times. How deeply Grandfather had loved Belicia. How a fire had burned down his first home. And then how a yellow fever epidemic had taken his wife and son, leaving him to raise two daughters.

"But that is all ancient history," Grandfather said. "We must look to the future. Pedro, whom do you pick in the Cincinnati-Boston game?" Grandfather loved baseball.

"The Reds should have an easy win," Pedro said. "Too bad the Great Bambino isn't in town."

"I agree." Grandfather patted Pedro's hand. "Babe Ruth! I watched his longest home run ever. April fourth, 1919, right here at Plant Field. The crack of the bat sounded like a pistol shot! The ball flew five hundred and eighty-seven feet."

Bella said, "I just read that a seventeen-year-old girl from Tennessee is pitching against Babe Ruth next month."

"You're making that up." Pedro jumped out of his chair and pushed Bella. "What does a girl know about baseball?"

"I can hit a ball farther than you." Bella pushed him back.

"Can not!"

"Settle down, children," Mama said.

"I'm not a child," Bella said.

"Then stop acting like one," Mama said.

"Bella's right, Pedro," Grandfather said. "The young pitcher's name is Jackie Mitchell."

"They'll slaughter her."

"Time will tell," Grandfather said.

Mama called, "Bella, would you please help me a moment?"

"Why don't you ever ask Pedro to help?" Bella asked. "Just because I'm a girl—"

"I need you now, Bella," Mama said.

"A woman's place is in the kitchen." Pedro smirked.

"Says who?" Bella pulled Pedro's ear as she started down the hall.

"Ow!" Pedro yelled. "I'm telling Mama on you."

"Go right ahead." Bella clenched her teeth. If only Jackie Mitchell could hold her own against Babe Ruth next month. That would teach Pedro not to brag so much.

CHAPTER 5
One-Way Bread

On Monday morning Bella woke to the clop of horses' hooves and the tinkling of glass as the milkman carried the bottles up the walk and left them on the front porch. Ybor City followed a rhythm that was as steady as the tidal flow of Hillsborough Bay. Ybor lived and breathed in the clink of milk bottles, the clump of the bread man's feet as he stuck his fresh loaf of Cuban bread on the nail beside the front door, and the sharp pick of the iceman chipping a block to fit the icebox.

When they needed ice, it was Bella's job to put a card labeled "25" in the window. That told the iceman to deliver a twenty-five-pound block. In the afternoon he used his tongs to swing the block onto his rubber-aproned back and carry it into their kitchen. During the summer, children clustered around his truck and begged for ice chips. Some neighbors had refrigerators, but Mama thought it cheaper to buy ice. She was also afraid of electricity.

Rocinante bleated loudly in the backyard. Bella dressed and hurried outside. She looked across the yard and smiled. "You again!" A gray mockingbird was perched on a branch above Rocinante's head, making goat sounds. The bird was a trickster that could imitate everything from a cat's meow to a siren.

Bella set out Rocinante's food and water. "You have a good breakfast, pretty girl." Bella ruffled her tiny ears. "And don't worry about that bad haircut. Your coat will grow out as good as new."

Bella milked the goat and carried the pail to the kitchen.

"Morning, dear," Mama said. "Would you get the bread for me?"

On the front porch she took their Cuban loaf from the nail. A single nail next to the door meant that they wanted fresh bread. Two nails meant they were ordering cheaper day-old bread. Mary's family always bought day-old, and Bella pretended not to notice the second nail by Mary's front door.

While the coffee water boiled, Bella sliced and buttered some bread for Grandfather. Then she poured a steaming mug of coffee and boiled milk and set it on a tray. Since Grandfather lived right down the block, Bella often took him breakfast on her way to school.

"Is that my morning angel?" Grandfather asked when he heard Bella coming up his front steps. Each morning

Grandfather rose before dawn, lit the kerosene lamp in the parlor, and reviewed his readings for the day. Many of Ybor's *lectores* lived in fancy homes, but Grandfather preferred a three-room *casita*. Though his salary was generous, he spent most of what he earned on Mama's rent, his books, restaurant meals, gifts for the children, club dues, and a morning shave at the barber. Any extra money went to support the Spanish revolution against the king.

Grandfather's parlor walls were bare except for the painting of Grandmother Belicia, a silver-framed wedding photograph of Bella's great-grandparents, and Belicia's Spanish shawl, which had hung on the wall as long as Bella could remember.

"Good morning," Bella said. Though Grandfather's clothes were always neat, his home was cluttered with books, magazines, and papers. A lifetime of collecting had left him with a library that was the envy of Ybor's scholars, and he could find any book immediately.

Bella set the tray on top of the *Gaceta* newspaper. "One-way bread," Grandfather said, "just as I like it." One-way bread was the name the waiters at the Columbia Restaurant gave bread that was buttered with one pass of the knife instead of the usual back-and-forth motion that scraped half the butter off.

"Have a seat." Besides his bookcases, the only furniture he owned consisted of a bed, a table, a bureau, a wicker rocker, and three straight-backed chairs.

"You could use another chair," Bella said, lifting a copy of Émile Zola's novel *Nana* from a chair before she sat down.

"A great thinker once said a man needs only three chairs: 'one for solitude, two for friendship, three for society.' "

"Is *Nana* a good book?"

"It depends." Grandfather took a taste of coffee and a big bite of bread. "Ah"—he smelled the brown crust—"bread is sacred food."

"What do you mean, 'It depends'?"

"Some like it. Some don't. Two workers in my factory once argued whether it was proper to read Zola with ladies present."

"Who won?" Bella asked.

"Neither, unfortunately." Grandfather took another sip of coffee. "That night they settled it with pistols."

"Over a novel?"

"Literary disagreements are serious in Ybor City. Sadly, they both died."

They were silent until Grandfather had taken his last sip of coffee. He wiped his mustache and said, "Delicious."

"I don't understand how you stay so thin," Bella teased. Grandfather not only had bread and coffee at home, but he also stopped for a second breakfast on his way to El Paraíso.

"Reading burns up lots of calories." Grandfather chuckled. Bella knew he was only half joking, because he performed with such energy. He and Bella often acted out scenes in books and plays, and he could change his voice to fit any character.

El Reloj tolled up the street. Bella kissed Grandfather and ran out the door to school.

Bella didn't have a chance to talk with Mary until they were walking home that afternoon.

"I hope I didn't ruin things on Saturday night," Mary said.

"Of course not! You can't help worrying about your father," Bella said.

A boy walked past and made a canary whistle at Mary's yellow shoes.

"You little twerp." Bella glared at him, then turned to Mary. "I hope the boys are more mature next year."

Bella and Mary took their time walking home. "Smell the guavas?" Mary asked.

Bella nodded and closed her eyes as she breathed in the steamy jungle scent of the nearby plant. "Did you talk to Tony today?" Mary had a crush on Tony Martino, but she changed her mind about boys so often that Bella said she belonged to a love-of-the-month club.

"I'm sure he noticed me this morning when I walked past the drinking fountain."

"I don't know what you see in him," Bella said.

"Muscles. And big brown eyes."

"He reminds me of Rocinante, the way he struts around showing off," Bella said.

"I can't argue with that," Mary laughed. "Maybe we should call him Pretty Boy Martino?"

"Next fall you'll have to keep your mind on the books when we're in high school," Bella said.

"You mean if we—"

"Don't say 'if.' In September we'll be walking up the steps of Hillsborough High School just like we've always promised ourselves."

When Bella finally arrived at their *casita*, Mama looked ready to scold her for being late. But when she noticed Bella's face, she said, "How are you, honey?"

"It's Mary. If her family can't pay their rent, they might have to move."

Mama took a bottle of milk from the icebox and poured a glass for Bella. "It must be hard with her father gone."

"She's still hoping he'll come home."

"If only our Dom—" Mama stopped.

"I know, Mama." Bella set down her glass and hugged Mama.

What if Mary had to leave? After losing Papa, Bella couldn't imagine another empty place in her heart.

CHAPTER 6
Sitting at the Ritz

"**I**n the ancient city of London, on a certain autumn day in the second quarter of the sixteenth century, a boy was born to a poor family of the name of Canty, who did not want him. On the same day another English child was born to a rich family of the name of Tudor, who did want him. All England wanted him too."

Bella stopped reading and tossed the book onto the bed. "I can't concentrate."

Mary had stopped by Bella's after school, and they were studying for a test on *The Prince and the Pauper*. "You can't expect to follow in her footsteps and become *La Lectura* if you don't practice." Mary looked up at the photo of Luisa Capetillo on the bedroom wall.

"I've been thinking about Luisa, and instead of being *La Lectura*, I want to be known as *El Lector*, like Grandfather."

"Good for you." Mary picked up the book and looked at the picture of Mark Twain on the cover. "I still can't get over how much he looks like your grandfather."

Bella nodded. "If he'd trimmed his hair and mustache, he'd be Grandfather's twin."

"I think we should do something special this weekend," Mary said.

"Like what?"

Mary smoothed the back of her frizzy head as she thought. "Let's take our sisters to the Ritz Theater."

"For the Saturday cartoon carnival?" Bella asked.

"Do you still have those ice cream tops?" Five Sealtest tops paid the dime admission to the cartoons at the Ritz.

"I've saved up enough to pay for us all," Bella said.

"Perfect," Mary said.

"Remember the fun we had at those cartoons?" Bella asked.

"I always thought I'd win that bike."

"Me too." Bella nodded. "I held my breath every time they spun the prize wheel. I could see myself pedaling that red Schwinn down Seventh Avenue."

"How many years did it take us to figure out the game was rigged and nobody was ever going to win?"

"The bike is so dusty you can't tell it's red," Bella said. "Maybe we believed because we wanted to keep on wishing?"

"What if it's just as silly for us to think we can go to high school when all our friends are going into the factories?" Mary said.

"No one has studied as hard as we have. We deserve to go."

When Mary and her sister, Carmen, stopped by Bella's *casita* on Saturday morning, Mary said, "I've got a surprise." She opened her palm and showed five streetcar tokens. "Mama found them in a drawer."

Isabel and Juanita jumped up and down. "We get to ride the trolley."

The girls ran to the corner and waited until the trolley creaked to a stop. As they climbed on board, Juanita stared at the flashing signal lights and the glass doors that opened and closed with a metallic bang. The cars were painted a dark green and trimmed with red. The brass railings shone brightly, and a warm electric smell filled the compartment.

Carmen touched a lacquered oak seat. "It's almost too pretty to sit on."

"And look at the grand uniform on the conductor." Juanita studied the smart cap and brass-buttoned jacket.

"Hang on," Mary said as the trolley jerked forward with a crackle of sparks and a creak of the wheels.

A few minutes later the girls lined up under the long Ritz Theater canopy to buy their tickets. Bella asked, "Who's going to win the bike today?"

"I am!" Juanita called.

Bella and Mary didn't have the heart to tell their sisters the game was rigged. Each time the prize wheel was spun, they all cheered for their ticket numbers.

When the girls started home, Bella glanced down a side street and saw a curly head. "Isn't that Pedro?"

He ducked out of sight. "I hope he isn't hanging around the nightclubs," Mary said. "We've all warned him."

"The trouble with boys"—Carmen blinked behind her thick glasses—"is they just don't listen."

The girls all laughed.

When Bella got home, Mama asked, "Did you have a nice time?"

"It was fun." Bella paused in the bedroom doorway. Julio slept soundly, while Mama sat in a straight-backed chair and crocheted a doily. Bella stared at Papa's belt, which hung right behind Mama.

Juanita yelled on the porch, "Stop pulling my hair!"

"Pedro must be home," Bella said.

Then Julio started to cry. "That boy," Mama sighed.

Before Mama could get up, Bella lifted Julio from his crib. "Hush now," she whispered, rocking him gently. He smiled as he quieted in her arms. If only Papa had lived to meet Julio. Bella was ready for the day when Julio would start to ask questions about what his papa had been like. She would make sure that he understood the true spirit of Domingo Lorente.

CHAPTER 7
The Silvertone 1100

Late Sunday afternoon Bella was sitting in the green wicker rocker on her front porch and thinking of how often she'd sat on Papa's lap in this same chair, listening to his stories. And when the neighbors strolled by, she'd leaned over the porch railing to wave and smile.

The street was quiet today. A soft hint of pink had begun to streak the eastern sky, and small birds chirped in the spiky fronds of the palmetto. Mama had gone to the park with Julio and the girls, and Pedro was reading the funny papers for the second time.

Grandfather had taught Pedro how to read by translating his favorite comic strips, *The Katzenjammer Kids* and *Dingle-*

hoofer und His Dog Adolph, into Spanish. Then Grandfather had Pedro read the English to him. These days Pedro could understand everything but the hardest words.

Pedro pushed the Katzenjammer comic into Bella's lap. "What's 'Vot der' mean?"

Before Bella could answer, a crackling voice filled the air, and Rocinante started bleating in the backyard. Next door a half dozen of José Navarro's friends stood on his porch, peering into his parlor. The voice was coming from inside.

Bella walked over. "Hi, Bella," said José's nephew, Carlos.

"What's going on?"

"My uncle just got—"

Carlos was drowned out by a blaring static voice: "Welcome to the melodic sounds of the Twilight Trio."

"José bought a radio?" Bella asked.

"Wowee!" Pedro was peeking into the parlor.

"It's not just any radio." Carlos pointed. "That's a Silvertone Model 1100."

Inside, José was kneeling in front of a large wooden cabinet and adjusting the tuning knob. "There we have it." José stood up and brushed his hands together.

Music was playing now, and the static had dropped to a hum in the background.

"You can stay." Carlos talked more loudly than he needed to.

"Really?" Pedro said.

"Sure," Carlos said. "How about you, Bella?"

Bella shook her head and walked to the backyard, where Rocinante was rubbing her nubby ears against the oak.

"That's only music, girl." Bella tickled the goat's chin and went back to the front porch. A radio! The new models cost more than seventy dollars. How could José, a janitor, afford one? Bella narrowed her eyes and thought. Mama said that José got extra money from a part-time job as Charlie Wall's handyman. Wall was a local gangster, and José did odd jobs for him, like sharpening the killing spurs Charlie tied on his fighting roosters. José had once bragged to Mama that he made more working a half day for Charlie than the cigar factory paid in a week.

Bella picked up a book. But who could read with that noise?

When Mama came home with Julio and the girls, Pedro ran up the sidewalk to meet them. "Can you hear the Silvertone? Can you?"

"What are you babbling about?" Mama set Julio down.

"The Navarros bought a radio."

"Really?" Juanita's eyes brightened.

"I'll show you." Pedro ran next door, with his sisters trailing behind.

When Pedro and the girls came home, Juanita asked, "Mama, can we get a radio too?"

"Just because our neighbors have a radio doesn't mean we can afford one."

"We wouldn't need a Silvertone," Pedro said. "Carlos told me a Majestic is only five dollars."

"He means five dollars down," Mama said. "Then you have to make payments every month for a whole year."

"If José can—"

"It's time for bed."

After the youngsters were settled in bed, Bella and Mama sat down on the porch. Mama got out her silver-handled hairbrush, undid Bella's braids, and brushed her hair, while Bella read a novel.

"Hard to concentrate?" Mama asked over the humming of the radio next door.

"It's like a bee buzzing around my head," Bella said. The last strollers had gone home, and the street was empty.

"This is my favorite time of the day." Mama sighed as she pulled the soft brush through Bella's long hair. "I love the peace and—"

"You can't say 'quiet' like you usually do," Bella said.

"No." Mama shook her head. "Not with that radio on."

Later, when Bella went inside, she caught a movement in Mama's bedroom. She stopped. "Why aren't you asleep?" Bella spoke quietly so she wouldn't wake Julio.

Pedro stood up behind the bed. He was wearing Papa's belt over his pajamas.

"Pedro?" Mama stepped past Bella.

Pedro said, "I like to put it on sometimes 'cause . . . I miss Papa."

Mama hugged him. "I know you do. I know." Mama helped him take the belt off. "Let me put that back where it belongs."

Bella felt a pang, watching Mama's eyes well up with tears as she hung Papa's belt on the wall.

The next morning Bella awoke to a train whistle. Every time she heard a train or saw a hobo walking down the tracks, she thought of Mary's father. The newspaper said that millions of men were hopping trains and hitchhiking across the country in search of work. Mary's father had to send money soon!

After the clattering of the train faded, Bella enjoyed the *oooh-ooo-oo* of a mourning dove calling from the magnolia. Whenever Julio slept late, the house was so peaceful.

As Bella was filling the washbasin, the radio crackled through the window, and she almost dropped the porcelain pitcher.

"Welcome to *Morning Cheer,*" a voice sang out.

"Not already," Bella groaned.

Julio woke up crying. "Your little brother is no radio fan either." Mama picked him up. "I'm going to speak with José about waiting until a decent hour to turn on that squawk box."

CHAPTER 8
Payday

On Saturday afternoon Bella stopped at El Paraíso to walk Grandfather home. She noticed that the small yellow blossoms on the paradise tree had begun to brown. That meant clusters of purple berries would soon be tempting the waxwings and jays.

Bella paused on the lawn and listened to the final reading of the day, a sonnet by Shakespeare that Grandfather had translated into Spanish: "Not marble, nor the gilded monuments / of princes, shall outlive this powerful rhyme . . ."

The stately words drifting out the windows suited the still, green afternoon. If only she could learn to read so grandly! Grandfather had told Bella, "At day's end I like to offer a short story or poem for the glad hearts to carry home." Bella often thought about the poem she would read at the end of her first day as a *lector.* For now she'd chosen John Donne's "Go and Catch a Falling Star."

Grandfather finished the sonnet to the clapping of *chavetas* on the benches, followed by the scraping of chairs being pushed back. It was payday, and everyone was eager to be on their way.

The first workers who came out the door were arguing union politics. One man said, "Weren't you listening to Señor García today? He explained it all." Bella stiffened. Could Grandfather's prolabor readings get him into trouble?

The week before, Lola had told them about rumors that the Ybor factory owners were thinking about removing the *lectores,* but Grandfather had only said, "I wouldn't be doing my job if the owners didn't get upset. They're always looking for a scapegoat to blame their union troubles on. If that's the game they want to play, I have broad shoulders."

As the factory emptied, it got noisy outside. From the time she was little, Bella had enjoyed watching the cigar rollers settle their weekly accounts. The *tabaqueros* were paid in cash, based on the number of cigars they rolled. An average worker made around twelve hundred cigars each week, but a man nicknamed Rapido Rodriguez finished as many as two thousand cigars.

Bella heard him over the crowd. "With less coffee drinking and more work you fellows could do as well."

"They don't put pockets in coffins." A short man jabbed Rapido in the ribs with his elbow.

Another man called, "Live well when you can, Rodriguez."

"Fools and their money are easily parted." Rapido stuffed his pay into his pocket. Unlike most cigar rollers, who wore white shirts and ties, Rodriguez came to work in the same tobacco-stained clothes every day. He even refused to spend money on a hat.

After each worker was paid, he stopped at a table set up in the shade of the paradise tree to pay Manuel, the *cafetero,* for the coffee he delivered three times each day. Curling petals fell from the branches onto Manuel's table. When Bella was little, she used to fill a cup with petals and take it home to Mama, who loved having "a scent of paradise" in her kitchen.

A man beside Manuel was collecting money to send to Spain to help the people fight for independence from the king. Any worker who refused to contribute his fair share was called a *fascista.* The only worse thing a cigar worker could be called was *rompehuelgas*—strikebreaker!

An elderly lady named Miss Margie also waited near the front door, with a coin box in her hands. As a young girl she'd been crippled by an accident in a cotton mill. But the generosity of the cigar workers allowed her to live in her own house.

The final stop for each man was Juan Fernandez, the *presidente de la lectura,* who collected Grandfather's weekly fee of twenty-five cents from the workers who understood Spanish.

Everyone wished Juan a pleasant weekend as they dropped their quarters into his cigar box, but one man shook his head. "You have no choice, Cesar," Juan said. "Since you listen to the *lector*'s readings, you must contribute to his salary."

"No money for the Spaniard," Cesar said. "Those rich Spaniards came to Cuba and stole my family's land."

"You can't work here if you don't follow the rules," Juan said.

"Rules!" The veins on Cesar's temples stood out. "What are rules but an excuse to enslave the workingman? What are rules but a reason for revolution?"

When Grandfather heard the commotion, he came outside and approached the table. Grandfather nodded at Cesar; then he said something to Juan. Juan frowned but said, "Very well," and waved Cesar along.

"Bella!" Grandfather said. "I must be on my way, *compadres.* It is not every day that a beautiful señorita is available to escort me home."

The men by the table stared at her. One whispered and another grinned. Was there something wrong with her? Bella folded her arms over her chest.

"Good afternoon, Princess." Juan tipped his hat to Bella. He'd called her Princess since she was a little girl.

Bella waved to Juan as she walked up to Grandfather. "What was that all about?"

"Cesar Hidalgo?"

Bella nodded.

"Cesar is new at El Paraíso, but I've worked with him at other factories. He claims that when the Hidalgo family lived in Cuba during the last century, Spanish occupiers stole their land. I'm Spanish, so he won't pay me."

"He's angry after all those years?" Bella asked. "And you had nothing to do with it!"

"He's a fiery spirit. As a young man Cesar fought beside José Martí during Cuba's revolt against Spain. He used some of his family fortune to finance the war."

"If he's rich, he should pay you your quarter," Bella said.

"With Cesar it's a matter of principle."

"Will they fire him?" Bella asked.

"Juan wanted him dismissed, but I pleaded his case. A man shouldn't be punished just because he disagrees with the established way of doing things."

"Even if it means you don't get paid?"

"What is money compared to an issue of honor?" Grandfather offered his arm to Bella. "Shall we promenade?"

The cigar workers smiled and tipped their hats as Grandfather and Bella started up the walk. For a moment she imagined she was wearing an elegant white dress and stepping onto a palm-lined boulevard lit by a golden sun.

CHAPTER 9
The Babe Is Caught Looking

"**B**ella." The voice sounded far away. Bella looked up and saw Mary plucking bright red seeds from the magnolia tree in her backyard. Why would the seed cones be open when it wasn't autumn? Bella walked closer. Her friend was dropping the seeds one by one and smiling. Bella looked at the ground. A man lay at Mary's feet. Each time a seed hit his white shirt it turned into a drop of blood.

Bella opened her mouth to scream. It was Papa!

"Bella, wake up." Mama touched her hand. "Would you feed Julio? He's been fussing since five."

The image of Papa lingered long after Bella opened her

eyes. "I'll be there in a minute." She sat up slowly. She'd been having the nightmare since the day she'd learned of Papa's murder. She sighed and began to dress.

Bella took care of Julio and then gave Rocinante her hay and water. As Bella looked up at the blossoms on the magnolia tree, she saw Papa's face. The goat bumped her leg. "Sorry, pretty girl. I'm still dreaming." Rocinante lifted her head at the word "pretty," and Bella knelt to pet her.

Back in the kitchen she asked, "Mama, what's the date?"

"April third. Why do you ask?"

"I've got to see Grandfather." Bella quickly buttered Grandfather's bread and stirred hot milk into his coffee.

"What can be so important?"

"I just need to check on something," Bella said.

"Has the paper come?" Bella called through Grandfather's open front door.

"No time to say good morning?"

Bella kissed his cheek. "Good morning, Grandfather. I wanted to see how the game turned out."

"Game?" Grandfather thought. "Of course. The young lady from Tennessee who pitched against Babe Ruth!"

Bella opened the sports page. "Here it is. She did it!" she squealed. "She struck out Ruth! And Gehrig, too!"

"She did! To be honest, I had my doubts," Grandfather said. "That should have been the headline for the day."

Bella set the paper on her lap. "I wish I had talent."

"You do. You read beautifully. I know you'll win a part in a play someday."

"But I want to do something great right now," Bella said.

"Good. I guarantee you'll find your way in time."

That evening after the supper dishes were dried, Juanita ran to Bella, as she always did. "Story time!"

"There's something special first." Bella ran to her room and brought back the article Grandfather had clipped out for her.

"I want to hear a story," Pedro said.

"This is even better," Bella said.

"Indeed it is." A deep voice rumbled at the back door.

"Grandpapa!" Isabel and Juanita ran forward to hug his leg.

"I don't want an article," Pedro said to Bella. "I want a story."

"Listen to your sister for a moment," Grandfather said, "and then I'll read you a story myself." He pulled a copy of *Treasure Island* from his jacket pocket.

"Pirates!" Pedro yelled.

Bella began, "Chattanooga, Tennessee. April second. Jackie Mitchell, a seventeen-year-old, making her debut in professional baseball, struck out Babe Ruth and Lou Gehrig today."

Pedro's eyes darkened. "A girl? Never!"

"Let me finish."

"It can't be true!"

"Look for yourself."

Pedro stuck his face close to the page.

"Amazing, isn't it? Are you ready for your story now?" Grandfather began reading about a mysterious old pirate named Long John Silver, and Isabel and Juanita sat up in their chairs and hugged their knees to their chests.

Just then static buzzed through the window. Grandfather stopped and marked his place with his finger. "What on earth?"

"It's José Navarro's new Silvertone 1100," Pedro said.

"Silvertone?" Grandfather frowned.

"A radio," Pedro said. "Have you ever heard anything so great?"

"How can a man think with that dreadful sound?" Grandfather walked over to the window. "Do you mind if I close this?"

"Go ahead," Mama said.

Grandfather read a few more sentences and stopped. He pulled out his handkerchief and dabbed his forehead. "It certainly is warm."

Mama nodded, fanning herself with a folded piece of paper.

"Can't we open the windows?" Pedro asked.

"Your grandfather prefers the quiet," Mama said.

"I should be getting home anyway," Grandfather said.

"Please stay a little longer," Bella said.

"I need to prepare for tomorrow's readings. Why don't you finish the chapter?" Grandfather handed Bella the book.

Pedro opened the window, and Bella began where Grandfather had left off. To drown out the radio, she pretended she was on a *lector*'s platform, projecting to the farthest corner of a crowded hall. The children's faces were intent as Bella read how Long John Silver pushed a wheelbarrow holding a sea chest up to the door of Jim Hawkins's inn, chanting: "Fifteen men on a dead man's chest—Yo ho ho, and a bottle of rum."

The drone of the radio soon faded into the background as Bella's voice brought to life the dark pirate's tales of shipwrecks, walking the plank, and hangings.

CHAPTER 10
La Resistencia Revisited

"I almost wish we'd move, so Papa could never find us again," Mary said. "Six months. Not a postcard. Not a nickel to help us out." Bella looked at the United States map Mary had taped on her bedroom wall. Stickpins showed the places from which her father had sent letters: Philadelphia, St. Louis, Denver, and finally, Livingston, Montana.

"You don't mean it," Bella said. "I'd give anything to have a hope of seeing my father again."

"I'm sorry." Mary squeezed Bella's hand. "But sometimes I could scream."

"You're mad now," Bella said, "but if he doesn't come home,

I can see you heading out to Livingston—wherever on earth that is—to track him down."

"You're probably right," Mary said.

"Let's go for a walk."

They headed up Eighteenth Street and turned east on Twelfth Avenue. The sun was dropping behind the trees when they reached the edge of town. "The moss looks like it's on fire." Bella admired the red light that filtered through the branches of a live oak. "Remember when we saw that green flash of light just before sunset at the beach?"

"Let's talk about important things," Mary said. "Like the way Tony Martino was staring at me during our spelling test."

"I thought you didn't like him anymore?"

"I looked up from my paper and those dreamy eyes were—" Mary stopped.

"What's wrong?" Bella asked.

Mary pointed to a hand-lettered sign that was nailed to a post straight ahead: NO LATINS OR DOGS ALLOWED.

"No Latins allowed." Mary hung her head. "Don't they know who founded this town?"

"Let's go." Bella pulled her along. "The Anglos and the KKK have put those signs up before. You've got to be tough."

"I feel like taking a hammer and smashing that board to pieces," Mary said.

"Grandfather just laughs at signs like that," Bella said.

"How can he?"

"He says anger gives the Klan and their kind a power they don't deserve."

"I still wish I had a hammer." Mary walked faster. "I'm surprised those idiots know how to spell *dog.*"

"I agree." Bella matched Mary's stride. "I'd like to smash them and their signs."

"Latin power!" Mary lifted Bella's hand and yelled, "Hip hip, hooray."

When Bella visited Grandfather later that week, he said, "We may have a battle here after the cigar workers vote."

"Aunt Lola says it will be the biggest election since the Resistencia strike vote in 1901."

"Did she tell you how the 1901 strike ended?"

Bella shook her head.

"The Resistencia walkout shut down the town. I thought the cigar companies would give in, but the Tampa businessmen formed a secret citizens' committee."

"Like they're threatening now?" Bella asked.

"Exactly," Grandfather said. "In the middle of the night a schooner steamed up the Hillsborough River. A group of thugs crept into town and kidnapped thirteen of the strike leaders. They hauled them to Honduras and stranded them on a deserted beach. The kidnappers told them: 'Be seen again in Tampa, and it means death.'"

"But that was against the law!"

"The police and politicians let the committee run the town. It made no difference that the wives of the kidnapped men wrote to the governor of Florida. Their appeal was ignored. The message was clear: tobacco companies are immune from the law."

A crackle came through the window. "Your neighbors have a radio too?"

"That blasted machine has been blaring for two days."

"The voices are so harsh," Bella said.

"The main problem with the radio is pace," Grandfather said. "It never gives the listener time to breathe. A skilled reader knows when to slow things down, and he knows how to match his material to his audience and the season."

"Like the way you change your readings during the day?"

"Exactly. Tolstoy is perfect for a brisk winter morning, while Cervantes, though he's a man for all seasons, shines best in the green hope of spring. Would you please close the window?"

Bella walked to the window and paused. "Do you hear what they're reading?"

"It's all gibberish to me," Grandfather said.

Bella raised the sash higher.

"I wanted you to shut it," Grandfather said.

"Just listen."

A singsong voice broke through the static:

During the whole of a dull, dark, and soundless day in the autumn of the year, when the clouds hung oppressively low in the heavens, I had been passing alone, on horseback, through a singularly dreary tract of country; and at length found myself, as the shades of evening drew on, within view of the melancholy House of Usher. . . .

"Edgar Allan Poe." Grandfather shook his head. "Destroying great literature. I'd rather have them play their jingles."

"You read Poe with so much more feeling," Bella said. "Even I could do better than that."

"Please, Bella. Close the window."

CHAPTER 11
Graduation Day

On the day when Bella graduated from eighth grade, Grandfather treated the whole family and Mary to dinner at the Columbia Restaurant. "Money is no object when it comes to honoring Bella's achievements," Grandfather said.

They got the royal treatment at the Columbia. Grandfather was a friend of Pijuan, the chef; Pepin, the headwaiter; and Gregorio Martínez, a waiter called El Rey, the King, because of his elegant manners.

"And how is Señorita Lorente tonight?" El Rey bowed to Bella. "Roberto has often spoken of your fine scholarship. And I must say that you bear a striking resemblance to your beautiful grandmother. I knew Belicia well."

Bella blushed as Grandfather beamed proudly at her.

Bella noticed that Aunt Lola studied El Rey as he walked away.

Lola said, "Now, there's a man with proper manners. Do you know if he's attached, Rosa?"

"Really, I'm sure you'll find out!" Mama laughed.

"It never hurts to ask." Lola winked at Bella and Mary.

"All I know about Gregorio is that he burst into the Columbia many years ago," Grandfather said. "Some men were after him—he never told me why. To disguise himself, he picked up a tray and began waiting on tables. The owner was so impressed with his style that he hired him on the spot."

Dessert was *Brazo Gitano,* a cinnamon-scented cake piled high with toasted meringue. Little Julio clapped his hands every time Bella gave him a taste.

Over coffee Grandfather gave Bella a leather-bound copy of *Don Quixote.* "This book was my father's most prized possession," he said. "He read it to *tabaqueros* in the top factories in Havana and Key West. I have two other editions at home, so you won't be depriving anyone of hearing the story."

"And I have a surprise for you too," Lola said.

Bella looked for a package. Would it be some embarrassing lingerie?

"I spoke with the manager at my factory," Lola said. "And he said he would be happy to give you a job. You'd have to start as a stemmer, but I'm sure you'd advance rapidly."

"I'd been hoping—" Not wanting to hurt Lola's feelings, Bella glanced at Mary. "Mary and I have always talked about going to high school."

"I know you two like to dream," Mama said, "but with money so short these days we have to be realistic."

"I'd be willing to help," Grandfather said.

"That is not your responsibility," Mama said. "And it's time this girl gets her head out of the clouds." She turned to Bella. "How many of your friends are going to high school?"

"But the cigar factory?" Bella thought of the blue smoke, the hot, humid air. Men spitting into cuspidors.

"What did I tell you?" Mary whispered to Bella.

"Would you prefer these?" Mama held up her hands. Her skin was red and chafed from laundry.

"If you'd only allow me—" Grandfather began, but Mama cut him off.

"Bella should be grateful that work is available in these hard times," she said. "Besides, in a short while a nice boy will come along and ask her to marry him."

"I want more out of life than just getting married," Bella said. She'd always tried to change Mama's old-fashioned ways.

"I can understand what Bella's saying," Lola said.

"Would you mind your own business for once?" Mama nearly shouted at her sister.

Bella was ready to say, "And what becomes of a woman when her man is taken from her, Mama? Just what does she do with her life then?"

But before Bella could talk, Mary touched her hand and gave her a look that said, "Fighting will get you nowhere."

The air was hot and still when Bella woke the next morning. She slipped out of bed, careful not to disturb her sisters, and poured some water into the washbasin. She splashed her face and patted it dry. Then she looked into the mirror above the dresser. When Grandfather told her she was as pretty as Grandmother Belicia, she'd always thought he was just being nice. Yet El Rey had said the same thing last night. Bella thought of the painting of Belicia that hung in Grandfather's parlor. She pursed her lips and frowned. Her eyes were too large, her chest was too flat, and her ears stuck out past her braids. Perhaps Grandfather had—

Just then José Navarro's radio started up, and Rocinante bleated mournfully in the backyard. Bella ran to quiet the goat before the noise woke Julio and the girls. But when she stepped into the kitchen, she realized the Navarros' house was silent. Had another neighbor bought a radio?

Bella walked onto the back porch and saw a flick of gray in the oak tree. The mockingbird was sitting on a branch above Rocinante and imitating the sound of radio static. Every time the bird made its crackling whistle, Rocinante bleated and rubbed her ears against the tree.

Bella marched over to Grandfather's with the breakfast tray clenched in her hands. She had an important question, but she told him about the mockingbird first.

"Those birds," he chuckled, setting his newspaper aside. "A mockingbird on our block used to do a perfect imitation of a rusty gate opening."

Stalling for time, Bella noticed the headline in the paper. "Is Scottsboro in the news again?" she asked. Scottsboro was an Alabama town where nine Negro boys—the youngest was only twelve—had been arrested for molesting two white women.

"I'm afraid so," Grandfather said. "Eight of the boys were sentenced to death."

"To death! That fast? How could they get a fair hearing?"

"The longest trial lasted only five hours."

"Do you think they're guilty?" Bella asked.

"It seems too quick and convenient," Grandfather said. "But I can tell you have more on your mind than the law."

"Does it show that much?"

Grandfather nodded.

"Will you do me a favor?"

"Of course."

"Help me convince Mama that I should go to school next fall," Bella said.

"Rosa is a proud woman." Grandfather set his cup down.

"She'd listen to you."

"Rosa sees your working as a way to keep her family independent. You know I've offered her money more times than I can count. And frankly I haven't saved much. It seems there's always a good book to buy or a cause to support."

"High school doesn't cost anything."

"But think of the wages you could earn. And your mother has to think of Pedro. He'll be ready for high school soon."

"Now you're sounding just like Mama. Pedro hates school. Why should he go and not me?" Bella couldn't believe what Grandfather was saying.

"As a man he'll have to support his family."

"But look at Mama," Bella said. "Think how much better off we'd be if she were more educated and hadn't been so dependent on Papa."

"Custom dictates that a man go to school first."

"Can't you at least talk to her? This is my whole future."

"As much as I'd like to help, it wouldn't be proper for me to interfere."

Bella felt her face redden. "Grandfather!" How could the man who had always been her champion think she was less important because she was a girl? "You know how much I love books. If I studied hard, I might even be able to go to college. I could become a *lector*, like you. You said there've been some fine women readers in the past."

"Luisa Capetillo was exceptional, of course. But—" Grandfather rubbed his fingers across his brow. "In truth, Bella, it's hard for a woman to make her way in a man's world. I'd hate to see you disappointed."

"I'll only be disappointed if I don't try. If Jackie Mitchell has the courage to stand up to Babe Ruth, shouldn't I at least be willing to take my chances at a lectern?"

"I know I've encouraged you to challenge yourself, but—"

"You've always told me that grand dreams are the seeds of grand deeds."

"But we must be practical, too."

She almost shouted, "Enough of this talk!" Instead, she said, "I'm going home."

"So soon?"

"Mama needs my help." Bella's mouth was tight as she started down the steps. She was furious. How could he say he was worried about her being disappointed, when she was more discouraged at this moment than she'd ever been in her life?

CHAPTER 12
Despalilladoras

The evening before Bella started work at the Rafael Fuente Factory, she and Mary decided to go for a walk. Bella was sitting on the porch with Mama and the girls when Mary arrived.

Bella jumped up. "I don't believe it!" Mary was wearing the same dress as always, but her yellow shoes were gone.

"What do you think?" Mary pushed her shiny black shoe forward as if she were modeling Cinderella's glass slipper.

Bella leaned down. "I can see my face in the shine."

"I bought them used from the shoemaker."

"They look brand-new," Bella said. "But how—"

"Did I get the money?"

Bella nodded.

"That's the best news! Father finally wrote!"

Bella gave Mary a hug. "How wonderful!" As happy as Bella was for Mary, she couldn't help feeling a little jealous.

"He got a job in Colorado on a big dam-building project."

"Hoover Dam?" Mother asked.

"Yes," Mary said. "The work is hot and dusty, but he's getting fifty cents an hour."

"That's good money!" Bella said.

"Your shoes are very pretty," Juanita said.

Mary smiled. "The minute I got these, I tossed the old yellow ones into the garbage."

As the girls strolled up the street past Ferlita's, Mary asked, "Is your mama still set on your working at the factory?"

"It wouldn't be so bad if I was just there for the summer."

"Maybe she'll change her mind?" Mary said. "My luck turned for the better, didn't it?"

"I'd love to be in school next fall when you get to show off your new shoes."

"Mama might keep me cleaning full-time. And if she doesn't, those boys will find something else to tease me about."

"They can be so mean," Bella agreed. "How is your job?"

Mary was helping her mother do housework for a rich family in Tampa. "It's not fair for a few people to have so much. Colonel Purcell's children throw more food in the garbage every day than we eat in a week."

"If only we could trade places."

"I know it sounds great," Mary said, "but they never seem happy. The kids whine and fight all day long."

The next morning Bella helped Mama start breakfast; then she got ready for work. Instead of going to the factory as she'd always dreamed—wearing a fine white dress and reading to the workers from a lectern—she had to put on her oldest dress and apron. And instead of sharing great literature, she'd be stuck in a stuffy room, stemming tobacco leaves. Bella felt like crying the whole way to Lola's house.

Lola opened her door with a big grin. "Today we'll see how good a *despalilladora* you are. If you don't stem those leaves just right, the cigar rollers will tan your hide."

"Really?"

"I'm joking. A monkey could pull out the stems and bunch the tobacco leaves together. But once you learn, you'll be promoted."

"So how did you start?"

"Like so many in the old days, I began as a *chinchal.*"

Bella frowned. *Chinchal* was one of the words for bedbug.

"It was a small household cigar factory. They called them *chinchales* because the people were packed into one place like bedbugs. We had twenty people working in a little house. Most everyone on our block helped. Even Rosa."

"Mama was a cigar roller?" Bella asked.

"Hasn't she ever told you?"

Bella shook her head.

"Rosa had a knack. She always had quicker hands than me."

"Why didn't she keep working?"

"A handsome young cigar roller named Domingo happened by one day, and she traded making cigars for making babies."

Bella blushed.

When they arrived at the Rafael Fuente Factory, Lola gave Bella a tour of the building before she introduced her to the supervisor.

Like most cigar factories, the Fuente building was three stories high. "The first floor is for sales, packing, and shipping. This early in the morning the only fellows around are the packers and the pickers."

A handsome man walked by. "Good morning, Miss Lola." He winked at Bella as he tipped his hat.

"Morning, Mike," Lola said.

"Do they all wear derby hats?" Bella asked.

"It shows they're the kings of the roost. Our main production starts on this floor too. In the casing room at the end of that hall"—Lola pointed down a narrow corridor—"men sort the leaves into the proper grades. After they dip the bunches in rainwater to soften the fibers, they send them up to the wrapper selectors and wrapper strippers on the second floor. That's where the important work happens."

"Is that by any chance where your rolling bench is?"

"I'll show you." Lola led the way up a creaky flight of stairs.

The light was dim, and the air had a damp, moldy smell. "How old is this building?" Bella stared at the worn places in the stair treads.

"She was built in 1897." Lola patted the open-stud wall.

As they entered the main workroom, Lola said, "We call this La Galera." She waved at a row of benches near the front. "I work under that window. And our *lector* sits there." Lola pointed toward the side of the long, narrow room. Unlike Grandfather's lectern, which was carved like a minister's pulpit, this platform was a simple stand with two-by-four railings. As plain as the lectern was, it thrilled Bella to imagine herself reading in such a huge hall.

"Two *lectores* share the reading," Lola said; and then, lowering her voice, she added, "but neither of them can hold a candle to your grandfather. Now I'll show you La Barbacoa."

"The barbecue?" Bella asked.

"That's the nickname they use for the room where we strip the binder tobacco. It gets a bit warm up on the third floor." Lola led the way up another flight of stairs. The air had a hot, bittersweet smell.

"You'll be right in here." Lola led Bella across the hall.

As they entered the stripping room, a husky man wearing an unbuttoned vest over a white shirt and tie said, "I see you've brought another pullet for my henhouse." One of his front teeth was solid gold, and he had a pencil-thin mustache.

"Good morning, Edgar." Then, turning to Bella, Lola said, "Meet your new boss, Mr. Mendez. Since Edgar has only women working as *despalilladoras,* he has the bad habit of calling them pullets and hens."

"Good morning, Mr. Mendez," Bella said.

"A pleasure to meet you." Edgar Mendez extended his hand. Bella reached out to shake the foreman's hand, but Lola slapped his hand away. "That won't be necessary," Lola said. "Just see that you take good care of my Bella."

"But of course." Edgar Mendez rubbed the back of his hand. "If you'll excuse me, I have some paperwork to do."

Lola chuckled after he left. "That grinning rooster and I go way back."

"But why did you—?"

"Edgar has a reputation for getting too familiar with his female workers, and I wanted to put him in his place," Lola said. "Don't let him try anything."

A young woman in a sleeveless white dress and a brown-stained apron popped through the door. "Is this the pretty niece you've been telling us about?"

"Say hi to Lorena Sanchez, Bella."

Lorena smiled. She looked only two or three years older than Bella. When Lorena reached out to shake Bella's hand, Lola said, "Lorena won't bite, sweetie."

"You haven't been slapping Mr. Handsy Mendez again, have you?" Lorena laughed.

"It was my duty to see that Bella got off to a good start." Lola patted Bella's arm.

"If you want to know anything about the cigar business," Lorena said, "just ask Lola."

"And if I don't know the answer I'll make something up. I'd better get down to my bench. Will you show her the ropes, Lorena?"

Bella studied the stripping room. The walls were bare brick, and the floor was puddled with water. Two dozen straight-backed chairs stood beside tables made out of planks laid across the tops of wooden barrels. One foggy window at the end of the room and four bare lightbulbs hanging from the center beam provided the only light.

"The work is simple enough," Lorena said. She picked up a damp tobacco leaf from the table and tore the stem loose.

"That's it?"

"All we do is strip the leaves and fold them into bunches. The job might be dull, but it puts food on the table. I don't even mind this year's production cuts. Working four days a week gives me more time with my children. I've got three little ones that my mama watches while I'm here."

"Have you worked a long time?"

"Five years. I started when I was thirteen."

"Good morning, Lorena," a voice called from the door.

"Hi, Ruby," Lorena said. "Meet the new girl." She turned to Bella. "You'd better put your apron on, honey."

By the end of the day Bella's back was aching and her fingers were raw from tugging on the slippery stems. Her hands were stained a dark brown. On the way home she asked Lola, "Will this tobacco juice ever come off?"

"It's a nice soft shade!"

"Thanks." Bella squinted in the bright June sun. She had a headache from breathing the mixture of damp, moldy air and stale cigar smoke that drifted in from the hall. But the biggest disappointment was not being able to hear the *lectores*. She'd hoped their voices would carry to the stripping room, but neither of the readers had enough *fuerza de grito* to project that far.

Luckily, most of the women in Lorena's crew turned out to

be good company. The conversation and joking across the tables made the mind-numbing work endurable.

"Did Edgar treat you well today?" Lola asked.

"The foreman? Oh, yes," Bella said. "He was very polite."

"He'll answer to me if he bothers you."

"Were the readings good today?"

"As I told you, Santo and Diaz aren't strong readers. But Santo did a fair job on a Victor Hugo story."

"What was the name of it?" Bella asked.

"The one about the priest and the boy who steals the loaf of bread and ends up spending nineteen years in jail."

"*Les Misérables.*" Bella sighed. "That's one of my favorites." She thought, *Not only will I be stuck in a sweaty stripping room all summer long, but I won't get to hear the stories that I love.*

CHAPTER 13
The First Man

Bella was exhausted at the end of each day, but the children still wanted their stories. One night she said, "Let's walk to the Regensburg tower and watch the clock."

Pedro wouldn't go, but Juanita and Isabel were excited. Bella led the girls up the street, thinking of the many times Papa had taken her to watch El Reloj toll in the redbrick tower. As they waited, Bella knelt and whispered, "Get ready," just as Papa had.

Boom, boom, boom... A flock of blackbirds rose from the trees across the street, and the girls squealed at each bright clang. When the tolling was over, Juanita said, "Now you can tell us a story on the way home."

"Yes!" Isabel said. "Pedro will be sorry he didn't come."

At the end of the week Bella was looking forward to picking up her pay envelope. But after donating a nickel to one charity, a dime to another, and paying the *cafetero* for her coffee breaks, she was left with only $3.40. She looked at the change in her hand and thought back to the huge piles of tobacco leaves she'd stripped that week.

As Bella headed out the door, Lola asked, "How does it feel to be a working girl?"

"It's nice to get paid, but I wonder how much the Fuente Company earned from my three dollars and forty cents?"

"More than you can imagine, dearie." Lola turned down the street toward home. "But you'd be making a lot less without the union fighting for you."

"We'd be starving like those miners in Kentu—"

"Señorita García. I must say you are looking most lovely today."

It was Cesar Hidalgo, the grumpy roller from El Paraíso. He smoothed the ends of his mustache and bowed to Lola.

"Don't waste your sweet talk on me, Cesar." Lola smiled.

"If only I were a poet and could do justice to your beauty," Cesar said.

"You're so full of it," Lola laughed. "Have a pleasant weekend."

"May you enjoy your holiday as well, señorita."

As they walked away, Bella whispered, "I thought he was always crabby."

"Cesar can get ornery, but he's always been kind to me."

"How do you know him?"

"I worked with him at the Cuesta-Rey factory. He was always running off at the mouth." She leaned closer to Bella. "Did you know he once shot a man in a duel?"

"Grandfather said he had a temper, but he never mentioned that."

"It started when Cesar and another man were arguing over Cuban politics at lunch," Lola said. "No one thought anything of it, but that evening both of them showed up downtown with pistols. Luckily they were poor shots. Cesar emptied his gun and only wounded the fellow's shoulder. The main casualty was a customer in Joe's Barbershop."

"The barbershop?" Bella frowned.

"Joe had just lathered up a customer when a stray bullet shot out his plate glass window. No one blamed Joe for slipping with his razor—he nearly took the man's ear off—but poor Joe was so shook up he had to quit barbering."

Bella's eyes were wide. "You're lucky Cesar likes you!"

When Bella got home she was still feeling discouraged about her pay. But when she gave Mama the money, the expression on Mama's face was worth all the sweat. "You must keep some for yourself," Mama said.

"It's my turn to help now."

"We'll put your money right here in the cupboard." Mama took a pint fruit jar and set it on a shelf. "What we don't spend on groceries I'll leave as an emergency fund."

"Maybe there'll be enough left to pay for school someday?"

"One never knows," Mama said.

"And if Pedro decides he doesn't want to go to school, we might have more than we need."

"As the future breadwinner of his family, Pedro will have no choice but to go to school or at least learn a trade."

"But that's not fair." Bella filled the basin to wash her hands.

"Why must you always question things?" Mama asked.

"You know I get the best grades in my class. What's wrong with asking for the world to be fair?" Bella scrubbed her hands as she spoke. "It would be nice if life turned out perfectly all the time. But not everyone gets married."

"Don't talk that way. Of course you'll get married."

"Aunt Lola's doing fine. What if I want to be like her? Or work in an office or teach?" Bella faced Mama as she dried her hands. "And look at what's happened to us. How can you ask me to count on a man supporting me? And a family?"

"Don't be cruel." Mama fought back tears. "I try to take good care of you."

"That's not what I mean! Of course you do."

"I do the best I can." Mama was crying now.

"I know! I know. I'm sorry, Mama." Bella gave her a hug.

It's no use, Bella thought. She didn't want to hurt Mama, but why couldn't she let Bella have her own chance? Maybe Mama looked on school as a thing that would take Bella away from her . . . the way the trip to Cuba had taken her Domingo?

When Bella told Grandfather about her first payday, he said, "Work is noble, but you must never forget that gold is worthless compared to the currency of honor."

"All I want is enough gold to get me through high school."

"With your natural beauty and the nice dresses that I've bought you, it should be easy for you to find a proper husband."

"It's sad that husbands can be bought so cheaply."

Grandfather started to say something, but he looked at Belicia's portrait on the wall and sighed instead.

The following morning Bella woke to the smell of coffee. She opened her eyes and saw Juanita staring down at her. "She's awake!" Juanita called.

Isabel stepped forward with a tray that held a slice of bread and a steaming cup of *café con leche*. "What's this?" Bella asked.

"We've made you breakfast in bed." Isabel smiled.

"It was the girls' idea," Mama said. "Since you've been working so hard, they wanted to let you sleep."

"What time is it?"

"Nine o'clock," Isabel said.

"We should get started on the laundry." Bella pushed the covers aside.

"You sit back," Mama said. "We're already half done."

"Yes," Juanita said, "enjoy your rest."

"How nice of you to take such good care of me," Bella said. The girls stood proudly.

Bella lay back and relaxed. This was the latest she had slept since Easter.

Later that afternoon the family was sitting in the parlor sharing the newspaper. As usual, the Navarros' radio was on.

José had been keeping the volume turned down since Mama had spoken with him, but Bella still had trouble reading with the noise in the background. Once the sun went down, the reception cleared up.

Bella enjoyed some of the music that played in the evening, but she didn't like the way the radio pushed the familiar sounds of Ybor into the background. The whistles from the train and the box factory, the clanging of the trolley bell, the calling of the *pirulí* man all sounded muted and far away.

The next morning after breakfast Pedro ran to Grandfather's and borrowed the Sunday *Tribune* so he could read the comics. Though Juanita couldn't read yet, she studied the society-page photos of blond girls in fancy dresses posing with teacups in their hands.

As Bella was reading the front page, Isabel looked over her shoulder at a picture of a woman standing beside an airplane. "Did Amelia Earhart set another record?"

"Yes. She flew to a new high-altitude record."

"Who cares?" Pedro didn't look up from his comic.

"You're still mad about that girl striking out Babe Ruth," Isabel said.

"I am not," Pedro said. "But I say girls are lousy pilots. Wait until Lucky Lindy gets his new plane. He'll break more records in a month than that Earhart dame could set in a year."

"Don't be so closed-minded!" Bella laughed.

"What's that mean?"

"A closed-minded person shuts his mind to new ideas,"

Bella said. "Get used to it. Women will soon be doing anything they want."

Pedro rolled his eyes.

"And now that women can vote, it's only a matter of time before we have a woman president in this country."

"That's right." Isabel lifted her chin. "And maybe you can grow up to marry a smart woman one day and live in the White House when she's president."

"Never." Pedro shook his head. "Besides, what does Bella know? She's only an old tobacco stripper."

"Pedro Lorente!" Mama said. "Show some respect."

Bella looked down at her brown-stained fingers. Maybe Pedro was right. What good was it for her to talk about women presidents and famous female pilots?

CHAPTER 14
Chinches

The next day Bella stopped by Lola's house on the way to work. Lola was sweeping the sidewalk, and despite the hot, muggy morning, she was whistling. "Bella! Are you ready for another day in La Barbacoa?" Lola leaned her broom against the porch steps.

Bella tried not to frown. Lola's voice was too loud this early in the morning. How could Lola be so cheerful after all the years she'd put in at a cigar bench?

"I'm sorry you had to start at the hottest time of the year," Lola said. "The stripping room is downright cozy in the winter."

"I suppose it would be," Bella said as they started up the street. But she'd be back in school by the fall. Somehow!

"Are you coming to our union meeting this week?" Lola asked.

"I should help Mama with her laundry orders," Bella said.

"The union is only as strong as its members." Lola walked so fast that Bella had to lengthen her stride to keep up. "And we've had a long struggle in Ybor. I helped organize the stemmers in my first factory. Management thought they could walk all over us just because we were women. It took a wildcat strike to bring the bosses around. The cigar rollers wouldn't support us until we shamed them by calling through the windows: 'Where are your skirts, *afeminados*?' "

"I'll try to come to a meeting soon."

"Are you just saying that to shut your auntie up?" Lola grinned and squeezed Bella's shoulders.

When Bella got home from work, Rocinante was so tired from the heat that she lay on her side under the shady oak and waited for Bella to come and pet her.

"Hi there, pretty girl." Bella knelt and ruffled Rocinante's chin whiskers. "You're smart to rest today." The goat sniffed Bella's fingers and shook her head. Bella laughed. "I don't like that tobacco smell either, but we've got to get used to it."

Bella looked longingly at the shade. There were no trees on the south side of her factory, and her chest felt heavy when she breathed in the hot, damp air.

Mary walked around the back of the house. "Hi!"

"You look as hot as I feel," Bella said.

"The streetcar was stuffy on the way back from the colonel's. Mrs. Purcell had us polishing her silver all day."

"At least you weren't roasting in La Barbacoa."

"I can't imagine how hot that third floor must be."

"When I look at the women who've worked in that factory for twenty years, I don't know how they can stand it."

"Did Lola talk you into going to the union meeting?" Mary asked.

"I can't make up my mind. Grandfather always preaches compromise and calm. And Mama says family is all that matters. But when I'm sweating in that stripping room for starvation wages, I can see why Lola believes in the union. For now, all I want is to see a movie."

"What's playing at the Ritz?" Mary asked.

"Dishonored."

"Marlene Dietrich!" Mary said.

"More fun than listening to a bunch of cigar workers argue."

"Lola will be upset that you're picking the petting pantry over the union hall."

"She'll get over it." Bella chuckled at the nickname for the movie theater. "And what good are the few pennies I earn at the factory if I can't have a little fun?"

After Mary had gone home, Bella helped fix supper. The heat from cooking made the house so warm that Bella led the children out onto the porch for their evening story. She didn't always have time to keep up with Grandfather's novels, so lately she'd been playing games. Sometimes she had the children pick three objects, and she wove them all into a tale. Other times they took turns telling one together. Tonight Bella said, "Who wants to pick a title for a story?"

Pedro raised his hand. "How about 'Tornado Soup'?"

Juanita giggled. "That's a good one."

After a moment, Bella said, "I've got it. Once upon a time in a castle by the sea, there lived a lonely king. He had no wife or children, and he was bored by everyone and everything. He never went on quests. He never slayed dragons. He took no pleasure in the nightly feast his servants laid out on a table that was twice as long as this *casita*." The children's eyes got big as Bella waved her hand to show the length of the table.

"One day a bearded stranger arrived, wearing a torn chef's hat and a ragged coat. He was carrying an enormous leather-bound book with mysterious writing on the cover. Storm clouds were gathering in the east. . . ."

When the story was done, Bella helped Mama tuck Juanita and Isabel into bed. As Bella and Mama walked to the kitchen, Mama said, "You have Grandfather's gift for telling a tale. How the children love listening to you!"

"I wasn't sure how I was going to work in both the soup and tornado," Bella laughed.

She went outside to see whether Rocinante had water for the night. Bella touched the magnolia. Even the tree bark felt warm tonight. "Sleep well." Bella patted Rocinante's head.

By the time Bella climbed into bed, she was so tired that she didn't even hear the radio next door. But just as she was dozing off, Juanita yelled "Ouch!" and slapped at herself.

"It's only a mosquito," Bella mumbled.

"No, it's not," Juanita said. "Light the lamp."

"Go back to sleep," Bella said.

"I feel something too," Isabel said.

Bella lit the lamp, and Mama came in to see what was wrong. As Mama pulled back the covers, Bella was ready to say, "See, it's nothing," when she saw a black bug.

"*Chinches!*" Bella said, and suddenly she was crying. "I've brought them home from the factory."

"It's not your fault," Mama said. "Those bugs crawl out of the tobacco bales. There's nothing you can do to keep them from getting onto your clothes. We'll just air things out tomorrow."

Airing things out took the better part of the next morning. Luckily, Bella had the day off. They began by taking the beds apart and carrying them to the backyard. Juanita had to stand on "goat watch" after Rocinante tried to chew the corner of one mattress. Next Mama lit a fire under the washtub. "While the water is heating, pick the bugs off the mattresses and throw them into the fire," she said. "And let's not make a spectacle of ourselves for the neighbors."

"Yuck." Juanita and Isabel frowned as they picked at the mattress.

But Pedro laughed as he tossed a handful of bugs into the fire and said, "Listen to them pop."

When Mrs. Navarro stepped onto her back porch, Mama whispered, "What did I tell you about keeping quiet?"

After the mattresses were free of bugs, Mama scrubbed them with Octagon soap and sprinkled on El Vampiro bug-killing powder. The final step was rubbing the iron bedsprings with kerosene and setting them on fire.

"I'm glad those bugs got fried," Juanita said as they washed off the blackened springs. Finally they carried the beds back into the house.

"I'd do anything to not have bugs in my bed," Isabel said.

But when Mama said, "We should be able to stay ahead of them if we clean the beds once a week," both girls looked ready to cry.

Bella shivered. The piles of tobacco leaves at her factory must be crawling with bugs!

CHAPTER 15
The Bolita Boys

On her days off Bella continued to help Mama with the laundry and housework. Though she didn't have time to bring Grandfather lunch every Saturday, she visited him as often as she could. She missed listening to his readings.

One morning as Bella and Lola were walking up the factory steps, Bella heard a faint buzzing. "A radio?"

"We'll see about that," Lola said.

In the cigar-rolling room they found Edgar Mendez adjusting the dial on a radio cabinet beneath the *lector*'s platform while a second man stapled an antenna wire to an overhead beam.

"What's going on?" Lola asked.

"Isn't it a lovely morning, señoritas?" Edgar walked up to Lola and tried to take her hand.

"Don't waste your charm on me, Edgar. What are you up to?"

"As you can see, we are installing a radio for the amusement of the workers."

"What about the *lectores*?" Lola asked.

"The owners decided that the cigar rollers would appreciate listening to the World Series games," Edgar said.

"And how convenient that there won't be a *lector* here to read the union news to us," Lola said.

That evening Bella stopped by Grandfather's house and told him about the radio. "Can you believe they would replace a man with a noise box like that?" she asked.

"There are fewer of us *lectores* all the time," Grandfather said.

"But think of the grand tradition."

"Change is the only constant these days." Grandfather looked toward the street. "Now that horses have given way to automobiles and iceboxes are being replaced by refrigerators, it's only a matter of time before the *lector* goes the way of the blacksmith and the iceman. Especially since the companies blame us for all their union troubles. When the committee has me read labor newsletters, El Paraíso owners act like I've written them myself."

"But the owners know there's no way to compare a reading like yours that makes the characters laugh and sing to the static of one of those—those infernal noise machines!"

Grandfather started chuckling.

"What's so funny?" Bella asked.

"You're sounding just like me."

Bella stopped. "I suppose I am."

"I've dedicated my life to books, and I'll continue to read as long as people want to hear me." Grandfather hugged Bella with one arm. "But values can change."

"They would never replace you."

"It will do no good to worry over it," Grandfather said. "Aren't you going to ask how the novel went today?"

"Are you still reading about Captain Nemo's adventures in *Twenty Thousand Leagues Under the Sea?*"

Later that week Lola stopped by the house and said to Mama, "You need to have a talk with your son."

"What's he done now?"

Lola pointed at Pedro. "Where were you yesterday afternoon?"

"I was with my friends," Pedro said.

"Downtown!" Lola said. "With the very boys I've warned you to stay clear of."

"They're not that bad," Pedro said.

"Those boys are up to their ears in *bolita.*"

"*Bolita!* Gambling!" Mama said. "Pedro, I swear I will hang myself if you dishonor this family one more time." She wagged a finger so close to Pedro's nose that he had to lean back. "How many times have I told you that you're judged by the company you keep? You stay clear of those *bolita* boys. A man who lies down with dogs will get up with fleas."

Bella had often heard about *bolita*, but she hadn't known how popular the game was until her second afternoon at the factory, when a man stopped by at coffee break to collect the daily *bolita* bets. Nearly everyone on her floor pitched in a nickel. When Bella hesitated, Ruby said, "What's the matter? You too good to have a little fun?"

"I don't believe in gambling," Bella said.

"Well, don't you be beggin' for a share of the jackpot when my number comes up," Ruby said.

Bella wanted to say, "If *bolita* is such a great way to get rich, why are you sitting in a sweat-stained dress in a smoky cigar factory earning a dollar a day?"

On the way home Bella asked Lola, "If gambling is illegal, how can they collect money out in the open like that?"

"The whole thing started when this was a frontier town. Vicente Ybor asked that gambling be allowed because there was nothing to keep the men occupied. But nowadays half the cops in this town are on the *bolita* payroll. And I've heard that plenty of the higher-ups in city hall are taking bribes too."

"Do you ever bet?" Bella asked.

Lola shook her head. Then she leaned toward Bella and whispered, "Just between you and me, I heard from a very reliable source that the whole thing is rigged."

"Did Nick tell you something?" Lola's former boyfriend, Nick, worked at the Lido nightclub.

"I'm not saying who told me, but it's easier than you'd think." Lola stopped talking as they passed an elderly lady who was watering her flowers. Then she continued. "They play the game by putting a hundred numbered wooden balls in a cloth bag and tossing it into the air. A catcher grabs one ball through the material and cuts it free. To fix the game a fellow steals a ball and fills it with lead. That way the catcher can feel the heaviest ball. If they're in a hurry they just put one ball in the freezer so it's easy to pick out through the cloth."

"Just like the owners of the movie theater—they trick the kids into thinking they can win that bike!" Bella said.

"The crooks know how to work a person," Lola said.

Bella nodded. "They tease everyone into building up their hopes, but it's all a lie."

CHAPTER 16
The Heat Wave

The following Monday night Bella was telling the girls the legend of the pirate Gasparilla when a knock came at the front door and a voice called, "Mrs. Lorente?"

Mama brushed back her hair and started down the hall.

"Maybe it's Tía Lola." Juanita ran after Mama.

Officer Burns stood with Pedro beside him. The policeman handed Pedro's slingshot to Mama. "Your boy has something to tell you, Mrs. Lorente."

"Didn't we just have a talk?" Mama demanded. Pedro refused to look her in the eye.

"It was only a joke." He stared at his feet.

"Explain yourself." Mama placed her hands on her hips.

"One of my friends dared me to shoot my slingshot at Cannella's cart horse."

"Luigi Cannella, that poor old vegetable man?" Mama's eyes filled with tears.

Pedro lowered his head farther.

"I'm sure he meant no harm, Mrs. Lorente. But the horse got hit in the flank, and it bolted. A few bushels of tomatoes and cucumbers spilled onto the street. And the rim of the wagon wheel was dented when it hit a rock."

"How could you?" Mama wrung her hands, but Pedro only shrugged.

Juanita let out a wail and began crying. Bella knelt and gave her a hug. "It'll be all right."

"No. No, it won't." Juanita cried even harder.

"The policeman won't hurt Pedro," Bella said.

"It's Mama. She's going to hang herself from the clothesline. I know she is."

"What did she say?" Officer Burns frowned.

"Nothing," Bella said. "She's just upset."

Mama turned to Officer Burns. "We'll pay for the damages, of course."

"I told Luigi that you'd make things right. But in the future, Mrs. Lorente, could you—"

"I assure you this will not happen again—will it, Pedro?"

"No, Mama." Pedro kept his eyes cast down.

Mama didn't cry until after Officer Burns had left. Bella hugged her tightly as they both wept. "Hasn't he learned that his conduct soils us all?" Mama gulped between her tears. "If only Domingo were here. Have I been such a bad mother?"

"Don't say that, Mama," Isabel said. "It's not your fault." She looked at Pedro. "See what you've done!"

Pedro's lip quivered as he, too, began to cry.

It took every penny of the family's emergency fund—eight dollars in all—to cover the cost of the ruined vegetables and to repair Mr. Cannella's wagon. Mary walked to the market with Bella to pay the money. On the way Mary showed Bella a postcard her father had sent from the Hoover Dam construction project. "He says it's a hundred and thirty-five degrees out there!" Mary said.

"I'd better stop complaining about the stripping room," Bella said.

"Workers are dying of heatstroke every day."

Mr. Cannella said, "Thank you so much for settling things so quickly."

"It was the least we could do." Bella hoped the woman at the front of the store wouldn't overhear their conversation.

"Let me give you some vegetables."

"You don't have to bother." Bella wanted to get out of the store as quickly as possible.

"I insist." Mr. Cannella opened a paper sack and walked to the bins near the door. "I have some choice tomatoes and onions today." Bella's face burned with embarrassment.

As Mary and Bella started down the street, Bella said, "I can't believe Pedro did this to me."

"You have to remember he's just a little boy," Mary said.

"I'll be spending the next twenty years in a cigar factory. And he gets to go to school!"

"Things are bound to improve soon."

"That's easy for you to say, Miss Shiny Shoes." Before the last word was out, Bella regretted what she'd said.

But it was too late. Mary looked as if Bella had slapped her. "I was only trying to help."

"I'm sorry." Bella reached out to take her hand, but Mary pulled away.

When Bella got home, Pedro met her at the door. "I promise to pay you back," he said. "I really will."

"Do you think I'm stupid enough to believe that? And you're the one who'll be going to school instead of me! I'll be stuck in that factory. It's not fair." Bella was just as angry at herself for being mean to Mary as she was at Pedro. She turned to Mama. "I'm wringing wet." Bella's dress was plastered to her back with sweat.

Mama noticed the sack in Bella's arms. "Did you have extra money to buy vegetables?"

"Mr. Cannella gave us a few tomatoes and onions."

"How nice of him," Mama said. "And did you tell him that Pedro would be coming over to help him load his wagon each morning for the rest of this month?"

Bella nodded.

"What?" Pedro said.

"It's time you learned responsibility, young man," Mama said. "I've decided that you have too much time on your hands."

As tired as Bella was, she couldn't get to sleep that night. Not only was she worried about Pedro and Mary, but the heat was also worse than it had been all summer. A breeze usually blew through the tall windows of their *casita* after dark, but tonight the air stayed dead calm.

Bella turned over, trying not to wake her sisters. A whistle blew as a freight train rumbled through downtown. She heard soft music from somewhere far away. She tried to take a deep breath, but the mosquito netting overhead felt suffocating. And Juanita's hot breath was wet and sticky on her shoulder. After listening to El Reloj toll twelve and then one o'clock, Bella tiptoed out to the porch with a blanket and a pillow and curled up in the green wicker rocker.

The following morning remained hot and still. As Bella took her seat at the worktable, the bitter scent of damp tobacco hung heavy in the air of La Barbacoa. Ruby said, "It didn't cool off one bit in here overnight."

"The air's so stale," Lorena said. "We need a sea breeze bad."

As the sun baked the roof, Bella heard the tin sheeting creak, expanding overhead. Ruby said, "If it gets any hotter my head's gonna catch on fire."

Bella was too tired to smile. Her hair and dress were soaked with sweat.

"You holding up okay, honey?" Lorena asked.

Bella nodded, peeling loose a tobacco stem for what seemed like the ten thousandth time that morning.

"Hades must be a heap cooler than this factory," Lorena said.

"At least you'll be feeling right at home if you ever have to pay Beelzebub a visit," Ruby said.

"Speak for yourself," Lorena said. "I plan on walking right through those pearly gates when my day comes."

"You be dreaming." Ruby smiled.

Luckily, a thunderstorm passed through Ybor just before quitting time. Bella took a deep breath of the cool afternoon air as she and Lola stepped outside. Thin trails of steam were rising from the wooden paving bricks on the street.

"I bet the temperature's dropped twenty degrees," Bella said.

"That will cool off the union hall for tonight's meeting," Lola said. "Are you coming?"

Bella eyed the cypress blocks in the street that had popped during the rain. "We'd better watch our step."

"You're changing the subject," Lola said.

"The union's doing just fine without me."

"You are the union."

"I really need to apologize to Mary tonight."

"You've been fighting?" Lola asked.

"I was rude to her," Bella said.

"Yes, say you're sorry," Lola said.

When Bella got home, Pedro walked into the backyard with a *La Gaceta* sack slung over his shoulder.

Oh, no—did he steal it? "What's this?"

"I've got a job peddling newspapers."

"Really?"

"I promised I'd pay you back that money," Pedro said.

"So you are a man of your word." Bella hugged him. "But don't hang around the nightclubs selling those."

"Would Papa have been proud of me for getting a job?"

"Absolutely," Bella said.

When Bella saw Grandfather the following evening, she said, "I'm sorry I haven't had a chance to visit lately."

"I would have been bad company in this heat." Grandfather fanned himself with the newspaper.

"How can you wear that suit coat all the time?"

"It's the *lector*'s uniform. So how does Pedro like his new job?"

"You heard already?"

"My friend Victor Manteiga owns *La Gaceta*. Tell Pedro he's doing an honorable thing." Grandfather fanned himself again. "So how is your electric *lector* working out at the factory?"

"The radio?" Bella smiled. "I can't hear the broadcasts in the stripping room, but Lola says the static is so bad that she feels like putting in earplugs."

Grandfather chuckled. "Maybe they'll decide that even a bad *lector* is better than one of those infernal noise boxes."

"A hundred radios couldn't replace you."

CHAPTER 17
The Pop Shooter

A week later, Bella was walking home from work when something sharp stung her from behind. "Ow!" She turned to see Pedro, crouched under a chinaberry tree, grinning. He had a pop shooter in his hand.

"You stop that!" Bella caught him in a headlock and rubbed her knuckles across the top of his head. "Now we're even," she said. "I should have known it was time for the pop shooter season."

Each August when the chinaberries were green and firm, the boys in town hollowed out bamboo stems. Then, holding the bamboo with a thread spool, they shoved a steel rod into the stem and pushed out the berry with a loud pop.

Pedro said, "You were such an easy target."

"Did you sell a lot of papers?" Bella looked at his sack.

"I did okay, but evening is the best time. I'll get rid of the rest later on. So what were you dreaming about?"

"How do you know I was dreaming?" Bella asked.

"You walked right by without even noticing me."

"I was thinking how much I'd like to go to school this fall."

"The paper said they're adding a junior college to the Hillsborough High building in October," Pedro said.

"So you're reading the papers?" Maybe he was beginning to grow up after all.

"It helps kill the time," Pedro said. "It's too bad Mama wants me to go to school. I'd rather work in a factory any day."

"If only she would see it that way."

"Race you home?" Pedro sprinted toward their *casita*.

"No fair!"

"Catch me if you can!" Pedro called.

Bella ran after him. It felt good to run hard. Her shoes pounded the hot, packed dirt, and her braids flew off her shoulders. She and Papa used to race from Ferlita's to their doorstep. The very last time they'd run home, Bella had lost by only a stride. Papa had panted and laughed at the same time. "I'll need to get into better shape if I want to keep up with you," he'd said. Bella had been sad to lose that day, but she'd been glad ever since that Papa had won their final race.

Now, Bella lengthened her stride, knowing she'd pass Pedro before they reached their yard.

CHAPTER 18
A Shopping Spree

On Saturday Lola stopped by. After passing out lollipops, she turned to Bella. "So how long have you been working now?"

"Going on three months," Bella said. "It feels like three years."

"It's time we treat you up with a shopping trip."

"We spend all my money for groceries." Bella looked at Mama.

"I've already talked with Rosa about this. It's been ages since you've had a new dress, and there's a big sale at Maas Brothers this week."

Bella hugged Lola. "A dress! Lorena did ask if I was going to the Halloween Ball at the Centro Asturiano."

"And you told her you had nothing to wear?" Lola said.

Bella nodded.

"It's your birthday next week! Your grandfather and I will buy you a new outfit—shoes and all."

Mama smiled and smoothed Bella's hair. "You've worked so hard. You deserve a treat."

Lola said, "Grab your purse, we're catching the trolley. This will be a girls' day out."

"To be young and have a figure like this." The salesclerk took Bella by both shoulders and looked her up and down. "A size six, I'd say. But those long legs are going to bring the hem up a bit."

"Good," Lola said. "We won't let Bella hide her best feature."

"A little advertising never hurts." The clerk patted Bella's hand. When Bella blushed, the clerk added, "You're a shy one. Unlike some of your relatives." She grinned at Lola as Bella fingered the sleeve of a gorgeous blue dress.

"Enough gabbing," Lola said. "We've got serious work to do."

For the next hour Lola and the salesclerk paraded Bella in and out of the dressing room, trying one outfit after another. Finally, when she walked out in a soft lavender dress, Lola shouted, "That's it! Perfect!"

The clerk cocked her head to one side. "That little number is the cat's pajamas."

Then the ladies helped Bella select a slip, a bra, and her first high-heeled shoes. Bella said, "You're spending too much money," but Lola only said, "Doesn't your grandfather say a thing worth doing is worth doing well?"

"Yes, but I don't think he meant it to apply to shopping."

"Shopping can be just as much an art as literature." Right then Lola noticed an imitation pearl necklace. "Look," she said, holding it up to Bella's throat. "A perfect contrast to your beautiful skin."

"It's darling," the clerk said.

"Now, we'd like a bag for her old things," Lola said. "This young lady is going to walk to the beauty shop in style."

"Beauty shop?" Bella asked.

"I took the liberty of making an appointment."

When they got outside, Bella said, "You've already spent way more than you should."

"I've been dying to see what that gorgeous black hair of yours would look like trimmed and styled."

"But—"

"It would be impolite to refuse a birthday present."

"Mary's not going to believe this!"

"Time for these to go." Lola's friend Lujuana unplaited Bella's braids and combed them out.

"Did you ask Ma—"

"No more braids!" Lola made a snipping motion with her fingers.

The whole time Lujuana was clipping and curling her hair, Bella tried to look into the mirror, but Lola said, "No peeking."

When she had finished, Lujuana said, "Now for a dab of rouge and powder and a touch of lipstick. There!" She spun the chair around.

"What do you think?" Lola squeezed Bella's hand.

Bella's jaw dropped when she saw the rich sheen of her chin-length hair. Her first thought was *I look like Grandmother Belicia!* but she said, "Where did my ears go? I look . . . so different."

Lujuana laughed as she flicked the chair cloth aside. "That's the object, honey. It'll grow on you."

"I love it!" Lola said. "Great job."

"She's a knockout for sure," Lujuana said.

As Bella crossed the street, her legs wobbled and she had to lean on Lola. Was it her new shoes? Or the shock of her new hair? She felt light-headed. When Bella glanced at her reflection in a store window, she saw herself standing taller. Could clothes make such a difference?

Lola said, "Before we catch the trolley, let's celebrate with a cup of *café con leche.*"

As Bella sat down in a sidewalk cafe, a low voice said, *"¡Que carne!"*

"See?" Lola whispered. "Those boys think you're pretty."

"No!" Could the hint of Belicia that she'd seen in the mirror be real?

"Look over your shoulder." Lola shaded her face with a menu as she spoke.

When Bella glanced behind her, a young man sitting with two friends tipped his hat and smiled at her.

As they walked up La Séptima, Bella concentrated on keeping her shoulders back and standing straight.

"That's my girl." Lola gave Bella's hand a squeeze. "Doesn't it feel great to get all dolled up?"

"Rosa!" Lola called up the porch steps. "Come see your new daughter."

When Mama came to the door she covered her mouth with both hands and gasped, "My, my." Tears filled her eyes.

"Ain't she a beaut?" Lola said.

"Bella!" Juanita shouted. "Is that you?"

"Do you like it, Mama?" Bella stepped toward her.

"I never expected—" Mama touched the back of Bella's hair. "I mean—it is very nice, but I'll need some time to get used to the new Bella."

"Me too, Mama! But so far, so good!"

CHAPTER 19
The Halloween Ball

On Monday morning Lola stopped by the stripping room. "So what do you ladies think of the new Miss Lorente?" she asked.

Lorena said, "I was just telling her that she's too cute to be wasting her time in this hothouse."

Bella blushed.

Edgar Mendez peered through the doorway. "I think she's pretty enough to go to Hollywood and try out for the pictures."

Lola turned. "The only thing you need to picture are these knuckles knocking you into next week if you bother my Bella."

The ladies laughed as Edgar retreated, shaking his head.

When Bella and Lola walked home from work that afternoon they passed a high school girl. Bella's eyes followed her as she turned into the library. "You're doing a poor job of pretending," Lola said.

"What do you mean?"

"I can tell you're dying to trade places with those kids."

"Oh..."

"You can't fool your auntie. But Rosa's right to not let Grandfather help. He hasn't saved a nickel for himself."

"What about all the money he's earned as a *lector*?"

"Everything he hasn't spent on you kids and his books, he's given to support the Spanish revolution," Lola said.

"He does joke about being owned by his books and his causes," Bella said.

"It's true," Lola said, "but he wouldn't have it any other way." She put her arm around Bella's shoulders as they walked. "I haven't told anyone this, but I've got a fruit jar at home just like Rosa does. And since I don't have Pedro burning up my savings like you folks do, my kitty is getting pretty full."

"Don't you believe in spending every dollar having fun?"

"I still have my fun money. You know a good life stretches the wrinkles?"

"So you've said." Bella chuckled.

"But I've managed to put a little aside. For you."

"Me?"

"I know how much you love books," Lola said. "I can't

understand it myself, but you've clearly got an itch to learn things. And I'd like to help you with your schooling."

Bella stopped and grabbed Lola.

Lola smiled. "I checked with the high school. They'd let you enroll at the next semester."

"Oh, Tía Lola!" Bella hugged her. "This is the nicest thing anyone has ever done for me."

"But for now we'll keep this our little secret."

"Can I tell Mary?"

"I'll leave that up to you."

Though Mama and Lola both wanted Bella to wear her new dress to the weekly dance at the Centro Asturiano Club, Bella decided to wait until the big Halloween Ball. Lorena had invited Bella and Mary to go to the ball with her youngest sister, Concetta. Since Lola had a Halloween party the same night, Lorena would chaperone the girls and loan Mary the gown she'd worn to her first formal dance.

Mary came over to Bella's to try on the dress. "You slip this on, honey"—Lorena opened her sewing box—"and Rosa and I will pin what we need to take in." But when Lorena and Mama stepped back to look at the silky blue dress, they both shook their heads.

"Does it look bad?" Mary was ready to cry.

"Just beautiful!" Mama said.

"Don't that take the cake," Lorena said, stepping forward and tugging gently at Mary's waist. "Perfect."

"You'd think it had been made special for her," Mama said.

"Colonel Purcell's daughter has one this same color." Mary

beamed. "You put your dress on too, Bella, so we can see how we'll both look."

In the days leading up to the Halloween Ball, Bella and Mary practiced dressing for the dance in Bella's bedroom. They wanted to wear their hair up, but Mary's kept springing out of the pins and combs. "I just hate my hair." Mary pulled at a tuft. "Maybe we could iron it to make it lie down?"

Bella laughed. "Don't complain. Mine is as limp as a noodle." Her hair popped loose from a bobby pin and slid down over her nose. "See what I mean?" Bella crossed her eyes.

Mary giggled. "Stop! I'm getting a side ache."

"I give up!" Bella yanked the pins from her hair and collapsed onto her bed, laughing.

On Halloween, Bella walked Isabel and Juanita home from a costume party. Finally it was time to get ready. She had just put on her new dress when Lola dashed up the back steps dressed in a devil's costume. "Have you heard the news?" she gasped.

Julio squealed and ran to Mama.

"I'm sorry, dearie," Lola said, taking off her pointy-eared cap and setting down her pitchfork. "It's only Tía Lola."

"What on earth is the matter?" Mama asked.

"The police arrested three men today." Lola paused to take a breath. "All union supporters."

"Who?" Mama asked.

"One was Lorena's brother, Hernando."

"Oh! Is he all right?" Bella asked.

"As far as I know"—Lola turned to Bella—"but I'm afraid Lorena and her sister are going to be busy tonight."

"There'll be other dances," Bella said. As disappointed as she was, she knew they couldn't go without a chaperone.

"But your dress is so beautiful!" Mama said.

"Are we ready to rumba?" Mary stepped through the back door. Then she saw Bella's face. "What's wrong?"

Mary looked crushed when she heard the news. After Lola had left, Mary said, "If we can't go to the dance, is it silly of me to want to try on Lorena's dress one more time anyway?"

"Of course not!" Bella said.

"You get dressed, Mary," Mama said, "and I'll make us all a cup of tea."

"Are you sure?" Bella knew that Mama only had a small tin of tea left over from the past Christmas.

"We'll have our own little party tonight," Mama said.

"Can we put on our pretty dresses too, Mama?" Juanita asked.

"You certainly can," Mama said. "I'll set the table while you're all getting dressed."

On Monday the factory was buzzing with news of the arrests. "Lorena," Lola asked, "how's Hernando doing?"

"He's holding up," Lorena said. "But poor Mr. Crawford!"

"I heard he was arrested." Lola nodded.

"Not Fredrick Crawford the house painter?" Bella asked.

"Isn't that a shocker?" Lorena shook her head. "A group of vigilantes knocked him unconscious and hauled him out to the woods. When he woke up they flogged him with leather straps."

"But why?" Bella asked.

"He made the mistake of standing up for Hernando and the cigar makers," Lola said.

"I heard that Crawford knows who beat him up"—Lorena paced toward the window and turned—"but he's not talking."

"Who can blame him?" Lola's eyes narrowed.

"The police will find who did it." Bella took Lorena's hand.

"Are you kidding? I'll bet the police were involved," Lola said.

Lorena clutched Bella's shoulder. "Everyone knows the sheriffs and police are all Klansmen."

"Let us know if there's anything we can do for Hernando," Bella said. It frightened her to think the police might be on the side of the Klan. Whom could a person trust?

When Bella visited Grandfather that evening, he'd heard about Mr. Crawford's beating.

"Have the police arrested anyone?" Bella asked.

"I suspect they never will."

"That's what Lola says."

"For once I have to agree with her."

"But those people should be in jail!" Bella said.

"If Crawford values his life, he'll keep quiet."

"But he doesn't even belong to the cigar workers' union."

"They wanted to send a warning to anyone who's thinking of supporting the cigar makers' cause." Grandfather sighed. "At times like this I wish we could go back to the old days. Back then we had to be wary of rattlesnake nests and alligator holes, but men maintained a sense of honor. I'd trade the vigilantes and the Klan for snakes and alligators any day."

On the way home Bella thought about how brave Lola was in supporting the union. She'd never understood that before. Grandfather's stories about labor struggles had always sounded like ancient history, but could the dark times that Grandfather feared be returning?

CHAPTER 20
The Labor Temple

Friday morning on the way to the factory, Aunt Lola told Bella, "We voted to hold a parade downtown to show we're united."

"Good!"

"We thought so, but the cigar companies convinced Mayor Chancey to deny our application for a permit."

"What about the right to free assembly?" Bella asked.

"Now you're talking like a union woman!"

"It isn't fair."

"Fairness has never held back a Tampa politician."

"What will you do?" Bella said.

"We're holding a protest meeting tomorrow at the Labor Temple."

"What time?"

Lola grinned. "Are you finally coming to a meeting?"

"There's no way the cigar companies should be able to stop us from holding a parade!"

"That's my girl!" Lola patted Bella on the shoulder.

On the way to the Labor Temple the next day, Bella and Lola met Officer Burns. "Isn't it a fine day for a stroll, Billy?" Lola asked.

Burns stopped and glanced behind him. Then he whispered, "It might be best to skip this meeting."

"I've never missed a union meeting in my life," Lola said.

"Don't say you haven't been warned," Burns said.

When they arrived at the entrance to the Labor Temple hall, policemen lined both sides of the street. "Are you sure there won't be trouble?" Bella asked.

"Don't worry." Lola took Bella's hand and led her down the sidewalk. Hundreds of noisy cigar workers were elbowing their way toward the front door.

Inside, Lorena said, "Can you believe all the cops out there?"

"I heard the mayor deputized a thousand American Legion men and war veterans to help control the crowd," Lola said.

"Now you tell me!" Bella said.

"Those fellows who are playing at being policemen scare me more than the regular cops," Lorena said.

"Isn't it great of Bella to support our cause?" Lola asked.

Lorena nodded. "So many of the young ones are unwilling to do their part these days."

"Is it always this crowded?" Bella shouted over the noise.

"It depends on how upset we are," Lola said.

As Lola and Bella walked down the aisle, they bumped into Cesar Hidalgo. Cesar smiled at Lola and smoothed back his hair. "Señorita García is looking lovelier than ever today."

"You keep playing the same tune, don't you, Cesar?" Lola chuckled.

As Lola and Bella took their seats, Lola said, "Look, *el presidente* speaks."

The union president stepped up to the podium. The workers all quieted, except for Cesar, who shouted, "I say it's time for revolution."

Someone yelled, "Pipe down."

"If the capitalists won't listen to reason, I say bullets will get their attention."

Lola whispered, "Let's hope Cesar hasn't been target practicing."

"Calm down, señor." The president rapped his gavel for order.

After the speeches were over, the cigar workers stepped out into the street. "We might not be allowed to parade," Lola said, "but we can stand together."

The flat crack of a pistol shot rang out. Someone screamed, and people ran in all directions. Bella stood in shock. Were the police firing on the crowd?

A man almost knocked Bella down, and a bottle smashed

onto the sidewalk. Men grabbed stones and bricks to throw at the police, who charged the crowd, swinging blackjacks and pistols. A man ran past, blood spattered on his white shirt.

"Let's get out of here." Lola pulled Bella closer.

Bella saw a heavyset policeman coming toward them.

"Look out!" Lorena yelled as the big man raised his blackjack over Bella's head.

"Don't touch her." Lola stepped in front of Bella and held up her hand.

"No!" Bella screamed.

The lead blackjack cracked down on the side of Lola's head. Bella and Lorena reached out to catch her, but she crumpled like a rag doll.

"Tía!" Bella dropped to her knees and touched her aunt's forehead.

Lorena knelt and pressed two fingers against Lola's wrist.

"Is she all right?"

"Don't you fret. Her pulse is fine," Lorena said. The police were chasing workers on all sides, and Bella heard Cesar yelling, "*¡Revolución! ¡Revolución!*"

Lola's face was ghostly white. Bella touched a wet spot above her temple. "She's bleeding!"

Lorena looked at the cut. "Run inside and get a damp towel!"

When Bella got back, Lola was sitting up. Though she looked dazed, the color was returning to her cheeks. Lorena took the towel and gently pressed it against Lola's head.

"I'm fine," Lola said, pushing the towel away and rocking forward to get up.

"Sit still," Lorena said. "You've got a little bump that needs to be looked after."

"There's one of 'em," a deep voice drawled.

Bella looked up. Two policemen loomed.

Lorena said, "She needs to see a doctor."

"The only thing she's gonna see is the inside of a jail."

"But she's hurt!"

"That's what happens when you throw bricks at an officer of the law."

"She never threw anything." Bella stood and pointed at the heavyset policeman. "You hit her with your club."

"That's not what I saw," he said. "It was a clear case of one communist rioter accidentally knocking out his buddy here with a hunk of brick." He nudged Lola's leg with the toe of his boot.

"Leave me alone!" Lola said. Blood had trickled down her cheek.

"We got us a live one, Cletis." The big policeman grinned.

The short man nodded and reached for the handcuffs on his belt. "I figured we might need these today."

"This woman has done nothing wrong!" Lorena stood up.

"Lucky we got us two sets of cuffs."

"Please!" Bella said. "She needs a doctor." She saw a familiar face out of the corner of her eye. "Officer Burns!"

"Billy will help us," Lola said. Her words were slurred as if she were waking up from a deep sleep.

"Officer Burns!" Bella called, pointing toward her aunt. "Lola needs—"

"Where's Billy?" Lola asked.

"He walked off like he never even saw me." Bella dropped her hand to her side.

"I told you they were all Klansmen," Lorena whispered to Bella.

Not Officer Burns! Not the man who'd always been so friendly. Bella faced the policemen. "You've got no right to arrest her."

One said, "We got us a bushel basket full of blabby women today." He bent over, snapped the handcuffs on Lola, and jerked her to her feet.

Bella shouted, "We told you, she's hurt!"

The short man stepped toward Bella and touched his black-jack to her chin. "Shut your face, missy, or we'll cuff you"—he nodded at Lorena—"and your scarecrow friend."

"You ignorant—" Lorena started toward the man.

"No, Lorena!" Lola cut her off. "You've got your children to think of." Lola took a shallow breath and leaned hard on Bella.

"It's not right!" Bella said.

"They have nothing to charge me with," Lola said.

"But—" Bella started.

"I'll be home by suppertime."

"That's smart, girls," the short man said. "I 'spect we'd a had to toss this little one back and let it grow up anyway." He leered at Bella.

Lorena clenched her fist and drew her arm back.

"Don't, Lorena!" Lola squinted as if she had a terrible headache.

With that the men led Lola across the street and pushed her into a patrol car.

CHAPTER 21
Grounds for Arrest

A week later Lola was still in jail. Grandfather and Mama visited her every day, but no matter how much Bella pleaded, she wasn't allowed to go. Mama said that a doctor had stitched Lola's cut, and her spirits were good. But Bella needed to see Lola herself.

No matter how many times the girls ran to the door, hoping that Tía Lola had been released on bail, the news was always the same.

Grandfather hired one of the best lawyers in South Florida, yet the court wouldn't even schedule a hearing. "The lawyer can't understand it," Grandfather said. "They have no grounds to hold her, yet they persist."

Bella had to do something. On Saturday, when Mama took the children to the park, Bella ran to Mary's house.

"I'm going to see Lola."

"You're not old enough to get in," Mary said as Bella led her back to her house.

"We'll see about that." Bella walked into her bedroom, where she'd laid out her new dress and shoes and had set some makeup on the night table.

Mary held up the nail polish. "Paris Mist?"

"I thought Lola would appreciate a present," Bella said.

"If we do your hair up like we'd planned for the Halloween Ball"—Mary lifted the back of Bella's hair and smiled—"you just might look old enough for this to work."

After Mary helped Bella with her hair and makeup, she said, "You look so pretty those guards won't want to let you go."

"Don't scare me," Bella said, slipping the dress over her head.

Bella picked up the nail polish, a lipstick, a movie magazine, and a notebook for Lola. Mary said, "I know something else Lola would like."

"What?"

"We'll stop by my house and get it," Mary said.

When Bella got off the trolley and looked up at the long rows of barred windows on the four-story brick jail, she felt like turning back. At the top of the center turret she saw the steel glint of a rifle barrel. Could the sights be trained on her? She stopped, but then she told herself, *After all Lola has done for me, the least I can do is try to visit.*

Then she remembered Mary's joke about the police keeping

her in jail. What if they made up a reason to arrest her? Maybe they'd put her in a special cell deep in the basement where they locked up girls who didn't listen to their mothers.

Bella braced herself. She opened the door and walked up to the desk. The elderly jailer wouldn't look up from his newspaper until Bella coughed.

"You want something?" He peered over his glasses.

"I'd like to see Lola García, please." Her voice trembled.

"We only allow adults." He turned back to the sports page.

"You don't understand," Bella said. "Lola's my aunt, and I really need to see her."

"Policy is policy." His head stayed down.

"I'm much older than I look. I really am." The man kept his eyes on the paper. "A minute wouldn't hurt, would it?" Silence.

Bella tapped her foot. "I'm not going to leave until I see her."

The man glared at Bella. Then he grabbed the keys from his desk and pushed his chair back. Was he going to lock her up? "How's a fellow supposed to read about the big Florida-Alabama football game?"

"I only need a short—"

"Fifteen minutes in the visitors' room." He pointed to a gray door. "I'll get her."

"Dearie, you are a sight for sore eyes." Lola hugged her. Bella was shocked. Lola's eyebrows were scraggly, and her eyes had black circles under them. Her tangled hair showed dark roots. Lola frowned. "How'd you talk your mother into letting you come?"

"She doesn't know. We'll have to keep it a secret."

"That's not right." Lola touched the red scar on her temple. "Promise me you won't try a stunt like this again."

"I just had to see you."

Lola stepped back. "My, my, we did pick out a lovely dress. Turn for me."

Bella spun and almost tipped over. "These heels are a terror," she giggled.

"Still not ready to rumba," Lola said.

"I've brought something for you," Bella said.

Lola smiled at the nail polish. "You remembered my favorite color." Then she looked at the notebook. "What's this for?"

"You need to write down every single injustice you've suffered," Bella said.

"Like your hero Luisa Capetillo did in her book?"

"You're my hero too." Bella hugged Lola. "Mary put something inside the notebook for you."

Lola's eyes lit up when she opened the cover. "Al Lopez!"

"That's Mary's favorite photo," Bella said.

"What a sweetheart. Now I'll have some company in my cell."

Despite Lola's carefree voice, her face was ashen. "Is your grandfather keeping you updated on the legal front?"

"He says you have a very good lawyer," Bella said.

"You should see the fancy suits he wears." Lola winked. "He must be costing your grandfather a lot of money. The good news is he's got great hopes for our hearing."

"They won't be able to keep you here. I'll testify to what I saw."

"I know you would, dear. But let's talk about happy things. How's Lorena doing?"

When Bella got home, Mama was waiting for her on the front porch. "I've been worried sick," Mama said. "Where have you been and why on earth are you all dressed up?"

"I went to see Lola."

"Don't tell me they let you in?"

"She was so glad to see me."

"That's no place for a young girl! Those wicked convicts!" Mama wrung her hands together.

"I never saw anyone but Lola, and she made me promise I wouldn't go there again."

"That's beside the point! Your grandfather is going to hear about this, young lady."

But when Grandfather arrived for dinner the next day, Mama must have decided that she didn't want to spoil the meal by worrying him, because she never said a word.

On November sixteenth Mama and Grandfather attended a hearing for Aunt Lola while Bella looked after the children. They waited anxiously through the afternoon. Bella was sitting at the kitchen table reading a story to Julio when he poked her in the arm and said, "Book, Bella."

"What?"

"Book." Julio slapped at the book in Bella's hand.

"Bad boy," Bella said.

Juanita said, "Don't blame him. You've been staring at that page forever without saying a word."

"I'm sorry, Julio." Bella hugged him.

"Did Tía Lola do something bad?" Juanita asked.

"Never!" Bella said.

Isabel said, "A boy at school said she tried to kill someone."

"She most certainly did not," Bella said. "The only thing your aunt did was stand up for what is right."

"Why'd they put her in jail, then?" Isabel asked.

"Sometimes people are accused of things that they don't do, but it takes time to prove their innocence. Once our lawyer speaks with the judge, everything should be all right."

Julio said, "Walk now."

Bella lifted Julio down from her lap. He trotted down the hall, and Bella hurried to keep up. When Julio turned into Mama's room, he said, "Belt," and touched Papa's worn leather belt. He reached up. "String."

Bella noticed a loose thread on the side stitching. She took the belt down and turned it over. The thread that held the pouch of tobacco seeds had been pulled loose. She spread the pocket open with her finger. It was empty. Her heart stopped.

Bella was waiting on the front porch when Mama and Grandfather returned.

Before Bella could ask, Mama shook her head.

Grandfather said, "I was hoping the prosecutors would realize their mistake and withdraw the case, but the judge ruled the charges too serious for bail. All fifteen cigar workers were charged with unlawful assembly, rioting, and attempted murder."

"Murder! Lola was just protecting me," Bella said. "The lawyer promised he could get her off."

"I've fired him," Grandfather said. "I'm getting an attorney from Tallahassee who's a labor expert."

"Won't that be expensive?" Bella asked.

"We have to do all we can," Grandfather said. "I didn't always agree with Lola's politics, but she doesn't deserve this." Grandfather's voice choked up, and Mama gave him a hug. "Lola has a little cash at her house, which should help start her new defense."

"But that was for—" Bella stopped.

"What?" Grandfather asked.

"Nothing," Bella said.

Bella didn't mention Papa's belt until Grandfather had left. "Have you sold the tobacco seeds to help pay for the lawyer?"

"Tobacco seeds?" Mama marched to the bedroom and grabbed the belt from its hook. "Pedro" was all she said when she saw the empty pocket. Then she slumped onto the bed, sobbing. "He'd been doing so well. What could have possessed him?"

Bella hugged Mama tightly.

When Mama cornered Pedro later that evening, he didn't lie. "I knew we needed money for Aunt Lola, and Bella wants to go to school, so—"

"So you stole from your own family?" Mama asked.

"A man who works at the Lido offered me fifty chances on *bolita*. With only a hundred numbers in the game, I thought that in a week or two I'd win for sure."

"Everyone thinks they'll win!" Mama said. "This is the last

straw! I should go outside and hang my—" She stopped suddenly and got so quiet that it scared Bella.

"Don't you know the game is rigged?" Bella asked.

"How?" Pedro looked confused as Mama cried silently.

"Do you think those *bolita* men get rich by being honest?" Bella asked. Tears ran down her cheeks. The tobacco seeds were gone forever, and with them Papa's hopes and dreams.

"But—" Pedro began.

"Have you ever seen a cigar worker living like the men who run the game downtown?" Mama said.

Pedro stood still. He stared at Mama. "I'm sorry," he said. "I was only trying to help." Now Pedro was crying too.

Shaking her head slowly, Mama stepped forward and hugged him.

"Won't it ever stop?" Bella put her head in her hands. She felt as if she was sinking into the same emptiness she'd felt in the black days that had followed Papa's death.

CHAPTER 22
Like a Thief in the Night

The next morning Mama didn't say a word about Papa's belt. Bella thought Pedro would be happy about getting off unpunished, but Mama's silence made him nervous. "What's Mama going to do to me?" he asked Bella.

She shook her head. "She hasn't said anything. I think you broke her heart. That's all she had left of Papa."

Thanksgiving was a sad time in the Lorente household. Bella kept thinking of ways to help Aunt Lola. She and her sisters and Mary wrote letters to the newspaper, and they circulated a petition demanding justice for the imprisoned cigar workers. Even grouchy Cesar Hidalgo signed it.

The best idea came from Isabel. "Why don't we dress up Rocinante with ribbons for the Thanksgiving Day parade and have her pull a wagon with a big sign that says 'FREE LOLA'?"

On the morning of the parade Bella and Mary helped the girls decorate the goat and wagon. Then they made their way to an alley near the official start of the parade. After a half-dozen floats had passed, Bella told the girls, "Go."

As the tippy little wagon wobbled out onto the street, the crowd pointed and waved. Everyone cheered, "*¡Liberación! ¡Liberación!*" Isabel petted Rocinante's neck. "Good girl. Everyone thinks you're so pretty."

At the word *pretty* Rocinante lifted her head and looked at the people lining La Séptima. She pranced forward like a proud show pony, and the cheers doubled. But halfway down the block a policeman stepped out and led the goat to the curb. As Bella ran over, she heard Juanita arguing with the officer: "You'll make our goat feel bad if you make her quit now."

"These young ladies worked so hard to—" Bella stopped. It was Billy Burns, the one who'd let them arrest Lola.

"It's you," Bella said.

"I had no choice," Burns said.

"You knew she was innocent. Now Lola's the one who has no choices!" Bella turned her back on Burns, then she helped the girls pull their wagon onto a side street. "At least people can read your sign on the way home."

The Thanksgiving meal was depressing. No one wanted to talk because every subject led back to Lola's troubles. And Isabel and Juanita were still sad about the parade.

"You tried your best." Grandfather took each of them on one knee. "It's my fault for not being able to get Lola out of jail."

"You can't help that the courts and police are crooked!" Bella said.

"I've preached justice my whole life, yet I'm powerless when it comes to getting a fair hearing for my own daughter."

The next day Bella woke early. After tending to Rocinante, she brought Grandfather breakfast. As she stepped outside with her tray, the sky was streaked with soft pink light. The air was cool, and small birds twittered on the grass beneath the palmetto. No one on the block had turned on a radio yet, so the old sounds of Ybor—the clang of the trolley and the whistle of the box factory—rang out pure and clear.

When Bella turned up Grandfather's walk, she saw his kerosene lantern glowing in the window. Just then a voice startled her from behind. "Bella Lorente, is that you?"

Juan Fernandez was running toward her. "Have you heard what's happened?" he called.

"They haven't hurt Aunt Lola!"

"It's the lecterns, Princess." Juan stopped to catch his breath.

"What?"

"Last night the citizens' committee ordered them torn out of the factories."

"No!" Bella nearly dropped her tray.

"Carpenters came in the middle of the night. By today every reading platform from West Tampa to Ybor will be gone."

"What's all the shouting out here?" Grandfather stepped onto the porch, holding a copy of *La Gaceta.*

"Señor García," Juan began. "I am afraid I must bring you bad news. I am very sorry to say this..." Juan paused a long time. "...but the lecterns have been removed from the factories."

Grandfather frowned. "All of them?"

"Yes, señor."

"It's so like those cowards to do their mischief at night."

"We'll fight them with all our hearts," Juan said. "They have no right to do this to you."

"I'm not the issue, Juan," Grandfather said. "Remind your people that this is not about the *lectores* but the workers' right to a free discussion of ideas."

"Well said as always, *Don Lector.*" Juan tipped his hat. "I must go and meet with the union officers." Then he turned to Bella. "Will you be coming to our special meeting at the Labor Temple later this morning?"

"I wouldn't miss it."

"In the meantime"—Grandfather nodded at the tray in Bella's hands—"my granddaughter and I have a breakfast to enjoy."

Grandfather took a seat and tried to smile. His hand trembled as he sipped his coffee.

"We've got to tell everyone!"

"That's up to the union. My job is to serve the members."

"I can speak up, because I'm the union," Bella said. "Tía Lola has always said so."

"Look where Lola's union got her." Grandfather sounded as if a great weight had been placed on his shoulders.

"Lola would want us to fight too," Bella said. "Your readings have been a gift to all of Ybor. And one day I hope to share stories of my own."

Bella expected Grandfather to argue, but he sat in silence. Finally, he looked into her face and smiled weakly. "Bold dreams are the province of youth."

The children were sitting down to breakfast when Bella got home. "You're going to be late for work," Mama said.

"No one is working today," Bella said.

"Why is that?" Mama frowned as she wiped Julio's face.

"The factory owners tore out the lecterns last night, and the union is holding a protest meeting."

"But not your grandfather's!"

"Juan Fernandez said every lectern in the city is gone."

"First Lola, then this." Mama clutched the edge of the sink and bit her lower lip. "We'd better watch out if the old saying is true: *No hay dos sin tres*—misfortune always come in threes."

"I think we've had our third misfortune, Mama," Isabel said.

"What?" Mama turned.

Isabel pointed at Julio, who had just tipped his oatmeal onto the floor.

By the time Bella arrived at the Labor Temple meeting, the street was crowded with cigar workers. The men, in their neat white shirts and ties, were grim. The gathering felt more like a funeral than a union meeting.

"Bella," a soft voice called.

She turned and saw Lorena.

"How's your grandpa doing, honey?" Lorena gave Bella a hug.

"He's more worried about Lola."

"Let's hope we can accomplish something," Lorena said as she and Bella took their seats.

Bella stood up. "I need to talk with someone." She started toward the stage. She'd been thinking about this all morning. Her legs felt weak as she climbed the steps. Even if it didn't work out, she had to try.

She approached the president and asked, "Would you mind if I said a few words about my aunt Lola?"

"As soon as I call the meeting to order, the podium is yours."

Moments later Bella found herself standing in front of a crowded auditorium. Her knees trembled. *What have I gotten myself into?* She tried to remember the speech she'd planned on the way over, but her mind was blank. The workers who had been so rowdy were now eerily quiet.

"Many of you know my aunt, Lola García." Bella's voice was shakier than her legs. As the crowd nodded, Bella reminded herself to breathe. "Three weeks ago Lola was standing outside this very hall. So were most of you." Bella found Lorena's eyes. "Without warning, the police charged us and clubbed Lola to the ground. She was arrested along with our other *compadres*.

Now the attackers have the nerve to charge these innocent men and women with assault!"

Cesar Hidalgo raised his fist and shouted, "A great injustice!"

"Not only do our friends remain in jail," Bella continued, "but last night those in power took it upon themselves to tear the lecterns out of our factories."

"More crimes!" a second man called.

"No matter how many platforms they rip down, the *lectores* cannot be silenced without our permission. For the voice of the *lectores* is our own voice. We must fight for the right of everyone to speak freely. And we must not rest until our friends are with us once again."

Bella was amazed when the crowd stood and applauded her.

At the end of the meeting, the cigar makers voted to hold a seventy-two-hour strike. Lorena turned to Bella as they made their way toward the front door. "Lola will be so proud when she hears about your speech."

"I can't remember a word I said."

"You were great." Lorena laughed. "And when we put seven thousand workers on the street, it should send a message to the owners."

"And the court will free Lola."

"Let's hope so."

Bella stepped outside, ready to duck if a pistol shot cracked over her head. Workers filled the street and spilled onto the lawns. When a newspaperman raised his camera to take a photo, everyone waved, and the man beside Bella clenched his hands over his head like a prizefighter. Luckily, there was no violence.

On the way home Bella was pleased to see that many of the shops were already closing to show their sympathy for the strikers. She stopped by Grandfather's house. "Not only have we walked out," she said, "but businesses all over town are shutting their doors to show their support."

"This doesn't bode well."

"But why?" Bella asked.

"Small businesses don't matter to the Anglo elite," Grandfather said.

"But if we stick together, the companies will have to agree to our terms."

"Things looked good for the cigar workers in 1910 until a group of vigilantes lynched two innocent Italian men in West Tampa." Grandfather shook his head. "The picture of those fellows hanging from a tree branch haunts me to this day."

"But surely if the workers are right—"

"Let's hope they're not dead right."

CHAPTER 23
The Lockout

O n the morning of November thirtieth the seventy-two-hour strike ended. Before Bella left for the factory, she went outside to feed and water Rocinante. To her surprise, Pedro was already filling the goat's watering pan.

"What are you doing up so early?" Bella asked.

"I thought I'd take care of Rocinante, since you have to get ready for work."

"How nice of you." Pedro was growing up at last.

Once Bella started up the street toward the factory, she was reminded of how much she missed Lola. Though Grandfather and Mama said Lola joked about how nice jail was, with its rent-free lodging and three square meals, Bella couldn't forget the sadness she'd seen in Lola's eyes.

As Bella turned the corner she saw a half-dozen workers standing by the factory steps.

"They locked us out," Lorena said.

"Why would they do that?" Bella asked.

Ruby said, "You remember how hard they pushed us before Thanksgiving?"

Bella nodded. "We had lots of Christmas orders."

"And we worked real hard to fill every one," Lorena said.

"So—" Bella said.

"So that means they won't have to worry about paying us for a good long while," Ruby said.

"Of all the low-down, dirty tricks . . ." Bella turned down the sidewalk toward home. Grandfather had said the factories would try anything. But losing her job right before Christmas? She felt as useless as the piles of soggy tobacco stems that she'd tossed on the floor of the stripping room.

Bella marched angrily up the street. What more could go wrong? She walked without caring in which direction she went. In her mind she kept ticking off the list of all she'd lost: Papa, Lola, the tobacco seeds, her job. The seeds! It was so unfair that her family's dreams could be taken away by the stupid mistake of one little boy.

It was time to stop feeling sorry for herself and do something. She walked down Fourteenth Street and stopped in front of the Lido. The casino was as quiet as a church that morning.

Freshly laundered tablecloths and towels hung on a clothesline out back, and the front door was open.

Bella stepped inside and waited while her eyes adjusted to the dim light. As the plush curtains, polished brass, and gilt mirrors came into focus, a low voice said, "May I help you, miss?"

Bella turned. The bartender was staring at her. She looked down and blushed when she realized she was still wearing her tobacco-stained apron and work dress. "I'm looking for Nick Bonnicotto."

"Help yourself." He pointed to a side room and went back to polishing a glass.

Bella stepped through the doorway and into an even darker room. "Is Nick here?" she asked. The room was empty except for a group of men at a table in the far corner.

One of them got up and walked toward her. "Who wants to know?" he asked.

"Nick." Bella was relieved. "You and my aunt Lola—"

"Hey," Nick said. "You're Lola's sister's kid. All growed up."

"That's right," Bella said. "I've come because my brother, Pedro, lost some tobacco seeds, and—"

"That ain't none of my business."

"But the seeds were my papa's dream. Now that he's gone—"

Nick dropped his voice to a whisper. "You'd better get if you know what's good for you."

Bella stood straight and proud, the way Lola had taught her. "Those seeds were all my family had left after my father was murdered. Murdered! And Pedro's just a kid. He didn't know any better. We don't deserve this."

"Look, kid—"

"Nicky boy," a gravelly voice called from the table. "What's the commotion?"

"No problem, Mr. C.," Nick called over his shoulder. Then he hissed at Bella, "These boys ain't nothing to mess with. You better—"

"C'mere, Nicky," the voice commanded.

After talking in low tones to the man at the table, Nick walked back to Bella. "Wait right here. And keep your mouth shut." He stepped into a side room. A minute later, he came back with the pouch of seeds.

"Thank you so much. Oh, thank you." Her hands were trembling.

"Keep it down!" Nick said. "You got no idea how lucky you are. If Mr. C. had been in a different mood, there's no telling what—" He pushed the pouch toward her. "Just get."

Bella didn't notice how hard her heart was beating until she stepped back outside. She felt dizzy as she squinted in the bright light. As she started up the sidewalk she realized that she'd just escaped from a place more dangerous than any jail.

Bella hurried home to share the good news with Mama. Halfway there, she heard the sound of an ax chopping.

When she reached El Paraíso she saw that two workmen were cutting down the paradise tree. One man held a saw while a second man tied a cable from the tree to the bumper of a truck.

As the man climbed into the truck and started the engine, Bella ran up. "You can't cut that tree down!"

"What?" The man cupped his hand behind his ear.

"You can't cut down the paradise tree. The factory was named after it."

"The owners want it gone. They're building an addition." The driver eased out the clutch. Once the cable tightened, the other man started pulling his saw across the base of the tree.

Bella sprinted up Grandfather's front steps. "How could they do it! How could they?"

"The paradise tree, you mean?" Grandfather put his book aside.

"You knew?"

"I didn't have the heart to tell you."

"How could they cut down such a beautiful tree?" Her eyes filled with tears.

"We're living in the age of the machine," Grandfather said.

"Did you hear we've been locked out of the Fuente factory?"

"They'll rehire the workers after the holidays. But at a reduced wage, of course."

"Then they'll bring the readers back too."

"We were removed because the owners needed to blame their labor troubles on someone."

"But you shared so many ideas!" Bella said.

"Ideas are what businessmen fear most. They pretend to believe in democracy, but they do everything in their power to crush it. In Cuba even the dictator Machado allows the *lectores* to denounce him and his policies."

"You belong at your lectern," Bella said. "And someday I'll stand at my own reading platform."

"The radio suits the factory owners. They want the workers entertained, not enlightened. And if they don't agree with the programs, they can buy the station and change them."

"But think of how much they'll be losing," Bella said.

Grandfather noticed the leather pouch in Bella's hand. "What's that?" She opened her hand. "The tobacco seeds!"

"I went to the Lido," Bella said.

"A miracle!" Grandfather said. "Though you never should have gone there on your own."

"I was so happy about the seeds," Bella said. "But now— That tree was so lovely." She stared at the pouch. "Why can't happiness ever last?"

"Don't let the tree spoil what you did." Grandfather reached for his hat. "We must tell your mother that you've brought back the seeds!"

CHAPTER 24
The Bread Nail

Bella woke to the smell of kerosene. She was shivering under the covers, and hungry. As happy as Mama had been at the return of the seeds, they didn't help put food on the table.

To make things worse, December brought the first cold spell of the season. Once they lit the parlor heater, a burnt, sulfurous smell filled the house and got into everyone's clothes and hair. As Bella climbed out of bed and dressed she could see her breath in the air. Ybor usually had only one or two days of freezing weather each winter, but since the *casitas* were built on pilings and poorly insulated, any cold was miserable.

Bella worried about Lola each day when she woke. Today she thought, *Dear Tía, I hope you're warm.*

Julio woke crying, and Bella bundled him in a blanket and carried him to the parlor before she dressed him. A short while later Juanita and Isabel scurried down the hall and huddled close to the heater as they slipped on their dresses. Pedro was already outside feeding Rocinante, who was frisky and happy in the cold.

After sending the children off to school, Bella walked to Grandfather's. He was frowning at the paper. "The mayor has authorized a secret committee of twenty-five to go after the union. The city council deputized special policemen to carry weapons. We can only hope that—"

Just then a knock came at the door. Grandfather looked up and saw Juan Fernandez. "Good morning, Juan. Please come in."

"I am afraid I bear more bad news, señor."

"I've heard about the police raid on union headquarters."

"There's more. The courts have issued an order banning the union. And they list two Spanish newspapers and a hundred and forty people—I am sorry to say that you are among them—who are forbidden from publishing 'seditious literature or speeches.' "

"Seditious?" Bella asked.

"Another way of saying I can't discuss the strike in public," Grandfather said.

"What about freedom of speech?" Bella asked.

"Freedom in Tampa is for a select few," Juan said.

After Juan had left, Grandfather set his coffee cup down. "I'm not in the mood for breakfast right now."

"Did you visit Lola yesterday?" Bella asked.

"She's amazing. So strong. But how long can she hold up if the court won't set a trial date?" Grandfather asked.

"They know they have no evidence."

"I can't believe it's come to this." Grandfather rubbed his forehead with his fingers. Bella had never seen him so discouraged.

He stared at his coffee cup. "After all the years I've searched for the proper voice to bring my stories to life. What do I have to show for it now but a house full of useless books? And my poor Lola . . . I've squandered my wealth for nothing but"—he touched a volume of Voltaire beside his chair—"empty ideas."

"Don't say that," Bella said. "Every worker in the city respects you so much."

As Bella hugged Grandfather, he looked at the painting of Belicia and said, "The companies have won the silence they've always wanted."

When Bella got home, Mama had a rusty hammer in her hand.

"There must be some other way," Bella said.

They looked at each other. "We have to eat." Mama handed the hammer and nail to Bella.

Bella walked to the front porch and tapped the second nail into the wooden siding next to the door. They were ordering day-old bread for the first time in Bella's life, and everyone in town would know how far the Lorentes had fallen.

CHAPTER 25
A Christmas Memory

On the morning of December eleventh, Bella was starting the fire under Mama's washtub when Lorena stopped by. "I just heard the factories are set to reopen on the fourteenth," she said.

"Under terms set by the citizens' committee?" Bella asked.

"We tried our best," Lorena said. "The good news is our whole crew, except for Ruby, has been rehired."

"Why not Ruby?"

"They labeled some workers agitators and laid them off."

"The committee!" Bella said.

"I know it's unfair," Lorena said. "I swear if it wasn't for having kids to feed I'd tell the owners to strip their own tobacco leaves. But with bills hanging over my head—"

"The layoffs have made it tough on everyone," Bella said. "Mama says Mr. Cannella is holding pages of unpaid accounts at his store."

"I can try to sell more papers," Pedro offered.

Bella gave Pedro a hug. "You've been helping as much as you can."

On the morning when Bella returned to work, she felt torn. Her family needed the money, but how could she support the factory owners who were trying to destroy Grandfather and Lola?

She and Mary had talked and talked about her choices. In the end Mary said, "You have to do what you think is right."

Bella rose early and made coffee. She heard the bread man on the front porch delivering their day-old loaf. The first thing she would do when she got home from work was take down the second nail beside the door.

On the way to the factory she buttoned up her sweater to block the breeze. Last night's ground fog still lingered in places, and the damp cold made her legs ache. Aunt Lola had always teased her when she complained about the cold. "Don't be a sissy," Lola would say. "Did I ever tell you about the winter I spent working at a cigar factory in Buffalo, New York?" And she'd go on to describe the handsome Jell-O salesman she'd met in the train depot.

As Bella neared the main entrance, she heard voices coming from the second floor. Could the rollers be at their benches this early? No—the radio. Bella stopped on the front steps. The voice was fast and choppy, clipping off the words.

"Is another one of my chickens coming home to roost?" a rough voice said. Edgar Mendez leered at her from the doorway, showing his shiny gold tooth. "You got wax in your ears, girl? I asked if you're coming in. I told the boss it wasn't your fault that your aunt and grandfather are radicals, and he agreed to save a place for you."

Bella turned around.

"Where are you going?" Edgar said.

"To visit a radical!" Bella said.

"Turn your back on us, and no factory will ever hire you." When Bella didn't answer, he yelled, "You're just as stubborn as that aunt of yours."

Bella lifted her chin high as she walked down the sidewalk. She was proud to be compared to Aunt Lola. Wasn't this the modern age, when all things were possible? If a woman like Amelia Earhart could set flying records, and if a young girl from Chattanooga could strike out Babe Ruth, then she could stand up to a cigar company.

Despite the cold, Bella began to walk slowly. It felt good to leave Edgar. But what if she'd done something stupid? Would her family end up suffering for her pride?

She soon found herself tapping lightly on Grandfather's door. "Is anyone home?"

Grandfather smiled. "Belicia," he said. "My morning angel. What a pleasant surprise. I thought you'd be returning to the fac—" Grandfather stopped when Bella's eyes filled with tears.

"I couldn't abide that Mendez man calling Tía Lola names."

"No person of principle could. The shameless ones who grovel before the bosses forget that even the brightest gold will tarnish—"

"—but honor shines ever brighter with the passing of time." Bella finished the sentence for him.

"Bravo!" Grandfather said, giving her a hug. "Now that you've rejoined the ranks of the unemployed, let's go to the Columbia Restaurant and celebrate with a second breakfast."

"But surely you can't afford—"

"When an event is worthy, no expense should be spared."

By late December, Grandfather had used up his savings to pay Lola's new lawyer. Whenever he was forced to sell more of his library to raise money, Bella got angry. "You've always said that books stand for the best hopes of men," she said. "Those crooks in city hall shouldn't be allowed to steal them from you!" And her own hopes for a career as *lector* faded with each book that was sold.

"I'm holding on to my favorite volumes, thanks to the pennies I'm earning from the column I'm writing for my friend at *La Gaceta*," Grandfather said.

When Bella stopped by Mary's that evening, she was surprised to see her friend wearing a turquoise necklace.

"From your father?" Bella asked.

Mary nodded. "It came this morning. I wasn't supposed to unwrap it until Christmas, but Mama let me."

"Things must be going well at Hoover Dam."

"It's so cold the workers have to build fires to keep from

freezing. But no one's dying of heatstroke like they did last summer."

"I'd take the cold over a hundred and thirty-five degrees any day," Bella said.

"Any news about Lola?"

"Grandfather's lawyer keeps asking the court to set a trial date, but they refuse," Bella said. "I brought her some Christmas cookies yesterday."

"Did you tell your mother?"

"We went together this time. And we found that Lola already had company."

"Her lawyer?" Mary asked.

"No," Bella said. "Cesar Hidalgo."

"The crazy cigar roller?"

"For once he was very polite. He'd brought her a cake."

"How'd she look?"

"Not quite as thin as last time, but she's still having trouble sleeping."

"That lawyer has got to get her out."

"That's my Christmas wish," Bella said.

On the morning of *Noche Buena*, Christmas Eve, Bella told the children a funny story about a Santa who dressed in black and traveled all over the world looking for bad boys and girls. When he found one he would swoop down and stick the child in his sack.

"I'll bet the black Santa is coming for Pedro tonight," Juanita said.

Pedro spent the afternoon tying cardboard reindeer antlers on Rocinante and hitching her to a wagon he labeled THE SANTA EXPRESS. Then he gave rides to all the children in the neighborhood. He made Julio a little kite, and Julio sat on Juanita's lap, holding the string tightly as Rocinante pulled the wagon up and down the street.

Grandfather surprised everyone by bringing a Serrano ham for their meal. Mama chided him for spending so much, but she looked happy as she sliced the ham thin and served it with small round potatoes. Dessert was espresso coffee, and the adults, along with Bella, sampled some *sidra,* a famous Asturian cider.

Later, when the bagpiper marched through town, Isabel said, "The piper was Tía Lola's favorite part of Christmas."

"Don't make me cry," Juanita said.

After the meal, Grandfather sat back in his chair. "Such fine fare reminds me of my first Christmas in Ybor."

"Wasn't the city all swamps and alligators back then?" Pedro asked as he and Isabel looked up from their dominoes game.

"Belicia and I had nothing, yet we had everything."

"How can that be?" Isabel asked.

"After a year of fighting mud and mosquitoes and yellow fever, good fortune came our way in December of 1886. Everyone was so discouraged that they were thinking of leaving town, but Vicente Ybor and his wife invited all the workers to their house for Christmas Eve. He said there would be a surprise.

"*Noche Buena* came at last. The guests arrived to find long tables set on the lawn in front of Ybor's mansion. Candles flickered, and Japanese lanterns swayed in the breeze. The tables sagged with jugs of wine and platters of roast pig, turkey, red snapper, and chicken. Then the servants carried out dishes heaped with yellow rice, black beans, yucca, and roasted potatoes. And a dessert table was piled with *turrónes*, walnuts, pecans, figs, grapes, watermelons, cantaloupes, and baked goods."

"So much," Juanita whispered.

"After the meal Ybor brought out a big box. He thanked everyone for their dedication. Then he announced his Christmas gift: 'In this box I have the profits from the past year. Each person who has worked at my factory will get an equal share. Let us enjoy *Noche Buena* as a family and pray for a prosperous New Year.'

"This was no small present, as everyone got a month's worth of wages. After a moment of shock, the workers cheered."

Mama shook her head. "How much the factory owners have changed!"

"We must hope that Aunt Lola returns to us soon. Soon!" Grandfather said.

"The finest gift," Bella nodded.

"Speaking of gifts," Grandfather said, "I met a man in a red suit earlier today." He walked down the front porch steps.

"You saw Santa?" Juanita leaned over the railing.

"Santa!" Julio clapped his hands.

"He introduced himself as Señor Santa Claus and told me that he'd left some presents." Grandfather reached behind the palmetto and drew out a pillowcase.

Back inside the parlor, he pulled out a paper sack and handed it to Mama. "This is for the whole family from Santa."

She peeked inside. "Roasted chestnuts. How did Santa know this is our favorite Christmas treat?"

"Hooray!" the children shouted, and Julio ran in a circle.

Next Grandfather handed each of the children a small package wrapped in newspaper and tied with a red yarn bow.

Bella asked, "You haven't sold more of your books?"

Grandfather lifted Julio onto his knee. "Why not, if the little ones can derive a bit of pleasure from the proceeds? My books are dead and dust."

"Don't talk that way," Bella said. "Your books have inspired more people than you can count."

"And I'll bet you'd like to borrow some of them when you start your career as *La Lectura*?"

"I want to be *El Lector* just like you."

"Ah!" Grandfather smiled. " 'Tis the season for wishing and dreaming."

CHAPTER 26
Stone Soup

By January Bella feared that she'd made a mistake by not returning to the factory. The number of cigar jobs in Ybor was at an all-time low, and fewer workers meant fewer laundry orders for Mama. Bella looked for another job, but men with families got the first chance at openings. And everything paid less than the dollar a day she'd earned as a *despalilladora*.

Many evenings there was nothing to eat but warmed-over coffee and dry bread. Mama saved money by buying bruised fruit at Cannella's and serving tiny portions of rice and beans. She even used the same coffee grounds three days in a row. At every meal she always took the smallest serving for herself.

The hardest thing was living so close to the giant brick

ovens of Ferlita's Bakery. "I wish there was some way to make that fresh bread smell go away," Isabel said.

"It makes me so hungry," Juanita said. "I feel like running over there and grabbing a loaf off the counter."

One night when Bella was cutting a few thin slices of bread to serve for supper, she caught a spicy smell coming from the Navarros' kitchen. "Mrs. Navarro must be frying chorizo sausages," Bella said.

Mama suddenly set a pot of water on the stove and clapped a lid on top. When the lid began to clatter, she said, "Open the window, Bella."

"It's cold outside." Steam had already formed on the inside of the glass.

"Do as I say."

As Bella lifted the window, Mama said in an extra-loud voice, "We will have a fine kettle of soup this evening."

Was Mama going crazy? There wasn't so much as a carrot or potato to throw in the pot. Then Bella heard the sausages sizzling on Mrs. Navarro's stove.

Mama's lips locked in a tight whisper. "I'm not about to let that woman know what the Lorente household has come to."

As firm as Mama's voice sounded, she began to cry.

"It's not your fault," Bella said, reaching out to hug her. "I should have swallowed my pride and kept my job."

"No one's to blame," Mama said. "The window, please."

As soon as the window was shut and the curtains were drawn, Mama cried freely. "First Lola and Pedro. Then the strike. And always—" She took a shaky breath. "And always there is Domingo. Here." She touched her bodice with her hand. "After all this time, I sometimes turn to speak with him as if he is still here."

Pedro called, "Is dinner ready yet?"

"I'm so sorry." Mama dabbed her eyes with a corner of her apron. "I try to be strong."

Bella hugged her. "You are strong."

As Pedro walked into the kitchen he peeked into the pot. "Soup?" he asked.

"No." Bella turned off the stove. "Bread and coffee."

"Again?" Pedro asked.

"Unless a fairy comes along with a magical stone to make us soup, bread and coffee will have to do," Bella said. "Did I ever tell you the story of stone soup?"

Pedro shook his head.

"Call Juanita and Isabel," Mama said. "Tonight Bella will start our meal off with a story."

The following afternoon Bella was washing the lunch dishes when the Navarros turned on their radio.

"Even the windows can't shut out that music," Mama said.

Bella nodded. But as she stepped away from the sink, the song stopped, and a man began reading a story: "True!—nervous—very, very dreadfully nervous I had been and am; but why will you say that I am mad?"

Bella raised the window partway so she could hear.

Mama frowned. "Yesterday you said it was too chilly to open the windows."

"I've heard this story before."

The voice was louder now: "The disease had sharpened my senses—not destroyed—not dulled them."

"It's Poe's 'The Tell-Tale Heart,'" Bella said. "A pitiful performance! Grandfather and I heard another man on the radio reading Poe just as poorly. Even I could do better than that."

"His voice does seem wrong," Mama said.

Bella slammed the window. "Grandfather says radio people should stick to their soap commercials and comedies." She dried the last dish and handed it to Mama. "If only—" She stopped.

"Yes?" Mama said.

"Why didn't I think of this before?" Bella set down the towel.

"You're not making sense."

"I've got to see Mary."

Mary opened her door as Bella ran up the walk. "Do you want to help me with a project?" Bella asked.

"As long as it's not cleaning," Mary said. "Mama and I just finished washing all the windows at Colonel Purcell's."

"Promise you won't laugh?"

Mary nodded.

"I want to audition for the radio."

"Are you serious?"

"So many of the performers are dreadful. If you helped me practice, I know I could do better."

"It might be fun."

"We could read stories and plays," Bella said.

"And commercials."

" 'Use Pepsodent twice a day.' "

" 'And see your dentist twice a year,' " Mary sang.

" 'This program has been brought to you by Pepsodent,' " Bella spoke in an extra-deep voice, " 'the amazing new liquid dentifrice that gives you a winning smile.' "

Both girls laughed.

For the next two weeks the girls practiced in Bella's or Mary's bedroom. Mary coached Bella as she read stories by Poe and Twain and Hawthorne. And together they made up silly commercials. Isabel and Juanita and Carmen had great fun pretending to be the studio audience.

One day Mary and Bella even sang a duet, pretending to be Olive Palmer and Paul Oliver, the stars of *The Palmolive Radio Hour*. Isabel and Juanita hummed along as Bella and Mary sang the Bing Crosby song: "Where the blue of the night meets the gold of the day . . ."

When they finished the last verse, Bella took the role of the announcer, but she got tongue-tied by the silly names: "Ladies and gentlemen, that was our resident songbirds, Palm Olive and Oliver Paul."

The girls laughed so hard that Mama came to the door and asked, "Is someone hurt in here?"

"We're fine, Mama." Bella was giggling so hard that she could barely talk.

"Too bad Lola can't hear us." Mary caught her breath.

"She'd think it was hilarious."

Mary raised her eyebrows.

"Are you thinking what I am?" Bella said.

"Do we dare?"

"The weekend jailer is a soft touch," Bella said.

On Saturday morning Lola grinned when she saw the girls. "I feel like I've won the daily double." She hugged them both. Her voice sounded hoarse, and she looked paler than ever.

After Lola had learned the good news about Mary's father, Bella said, "We've got a surprise for you, Tía Lola."

"Are you hiding a handsome man somewhere?" Lola looked toward the door.

"No." Bella shook her head. "But we've been practicing a few tunes." She nodded to Mary. "Ready?"

The girls sang their favorite song from *The Palmolive Radio Hour*. Then, while Lola was still laughing, they sang a Coca-Cola jingle they'd made up. After starting with the Coke slogan, "Meet me at the soda fountain," they added a string of silly rhymes like "It's too foggy on this mountain" and "I don't think you should be shoutin'."

In the middle of their song the jailer and a guard stopped in the doorway to listen, and the men both joined Lola when she applauded at the end.

Bella and Mary curtsied.

"You two should be on the radio," Lola said. "I'd much rather hear you sing than those silly Ipana Troubadours!"

Later that week Bella read a story to Mary called "The Minister's Black Veil." When Bella was done, Mary just stared.

"Was it bad?" Bella asked.

"No, it was very good," Mary said. "I could imagine that scary mask over his face. You probably think Lola was joking the other day, but I really believe you're good enough to be on the radio."

"Too bad I'm not a little older," Bella said. "I might have a chance of getting a part."

"When you add in being a girl and Spanish, the odds must be a million to one against you."

"If only we could talk Grandfather into auditioning."

"He hates the radio," Mary said.

"But think of how exciting it would be to hear his voice broadcast—" Bella stopped.

"What?"

"It might just work." Bella spoke slowly as she thought.

"Tell me what you're thinking!"

"What if we didn't give Grandfather a choice?" Bella said.

"Do you plan on kidnapping him?" Mary asked.

"No." Bella smiled. "But if I went to the station . . . I have an idea."

"You're dreaming."

"We'll see," Bella said. "Are you busy tomorrow?"

CHAPTER 27
WIAM

The following morning, after Bella had helped Mama hang out the clothes, she walked to Mary's with her new dress, shoes, and pearls in a paper sack, and a coin for trolley fare that she'd borrowed from the emergency jar.

As Mary helped Bella put on her makeup and pin up her hair, she said, "I may as well become a hairdresser, with all the practice I'm getting."

When Mary walked Bella to the corner to catch the trolley, two separate boys whistled. "Someone approves of my work." Mary giggled.

"The second one was whistling at you," Bella said. "And he's cuter than that stuck-up Tony of yours."

"If only Tony was mine." Mary sighed.

On the trolley ride into Tampa, Bella practiced her speech to herself. "My name is Bella Lorente." She imagined shaking the manager's hand. "My grandfather and I would like to read on the radio. I'm a storyteller, and my grandfather is the greatest *lector* in all of Ybor." But even if the station agreed to an audition, could she convince Grandfather to come?

Bella expected that WTAM Radio would be in a brand-new building, but she found the station on the ground floor of an old hotel. Except for the rear parking lot, which held a steel broadcast tower and guy wires that extended high above the roof, the office was an ordinary four-story brick building. Tall aluminum letters above the front entrance read W T A M, THE VOICE OF TAMPA BAY.

A cold breeze blew off the salt marsh at the edge of town and made her shiver. What would Grandfather say if he saw her now? How could she approach the very men who were trying to replace the proud legacy of the *lector*? But she had no choice.

To succeed in the Anglos' world she must be bold, like Aunt Lola, instead of letting other people control her life, like Mama!

Bella held her breath and opened the heavy glass door. To make the lobby look modern, fluorescent lights had been hung from the high ceiling, and the walls had been painted silver gray. The furniture was made of chromed tubes and stiff black cushions.

A secretary sat behind a long counter, typing. Bella had to say "Excuse me" before she turned.

"Yes?" the secretary said, keeping one eye on her type-writer.

"Could I—" Bella reminded herself to stand straight and proud, as Lola had taught her. "I mean, may I speak to the manager?"

"Do you have an appointment?"

"No."

"He's a real busy fellow," the secretary said.

"I understand," Bella said, "but my grandfather and I would like to read on the radio."

"You can fill out an application." The secretary handed Bella a form and turned back to her typewriter.

Bella stared at the paper. Grandfather would never submit to the indignity of filling out an application. "But you don't understand," Bella said. "My grandfather is a *lector.*"

"There's lots of folks who want to be on the air." The secretary began typing. "If he's serious, just have him fill out—"

"What have we here?" A handsome young man walked toward Bella. He was wearing a brown suit and polished two-toned shoes. "Hi there." He leaned on the counter. "I'll bet you're a dancer."

"No." Bella blushed and smoothed the front of her dress.

"Well, you've certainly got a dancer's legs." He shook Bella's hand. "I'm Jim Parsons, the assistant manager."

"Nice to meet you." Bella smiled and looked him in the eye.

"You must be a singer, then," Parsons said. "If your voice is half as pretty as your face, I'll see that you get your very own show." The secretary rolled her eyes and went back to work. "So what's your name?"

"Bella Lorente. But—"

"Say no more. Bella, Bella." He ran his hand through his slicked-back blond hair. "I have it. Spanish, correct?"

"Yes, but—"

"I have the perfect billing: Bella Lorente, the Spanish Songstress."

Bella laughed.

"No good?" the young man said.

"I'm not a singer."

"So I'm all wet?" Parsons stopped.

"I'm here because my grandfather—"

"We're looking for fresh programming, Miss Lorente."

"Both my grandfather and I would like to perform on the radio. I tell stories and he is a *lector*—the most famous reader in all of Ybor City."

"*¿Comprende español?*"

"Yes, and Grandfather's grammar and diction are perfect."

"We don't care about technical stuff."

"My grandfather makes his living reading stories, and he's taught me well."

"Well, we've been tinkering with the idea of a Spanish story hour. We may make it a regular feature. You and your grandpa should try out."

"That would be wonderful," Bella said.

"Bring him down here on Thursday afternoon, and I'll see that the boss gives you an audition."

Bella was so excited to tell Mama the news that she went straight home without changing her clothes. When she walked in the back door, Mama cried, "You've gone to the jail again!"

"No, Mama. I went to WTAM Radio."

After Bella explained her plan, Mama only said, "You're so smart! But Grandfather will never go near the radio station."

"He's got to at least try!"

The next morning Bella stopped at the market and Ferlita's and brought Grandfather breakfast. He looked at the tray without interest until he saw the butter. "One-way bread?" he said. "Have you forgotten there's a Depression going on?"

"I made a trip to the bakery."

"Can it be my birthday?"

"No, but I took a ride on the trolley yesterday, and I have some good news for you."

Grandfather smelled his bread. "What sort of news?"

"I visited WTAM Radio, and they want us to audition for their new Spanish story program."

"The radio!" Grandfather set his bread down and stared at Bella. "Have you lost your mind?"

"If you can hold the attention of a hall filled with cigar workers, it will be a hundred times easier to talk into a microphone."

"But I know nothing of those machines. The very thought of my voice flying through the air makes me dizzy."

"Don't the people of Ybor deserve to have literature performed properly?" Bella asked.

"But the *radio*?"

"Imagine what a help the extra money would be in paying

Lola's lawyer. Not to mention food for the little ones. It hurts so much to see them go hungry."

Grandfather sighed deeply and looked at his hands.

"I told them we were a team," Bella said. "Would you do it for me?"

"For you?" He sat up and took her hand. "Yes, my dear, for you and the family I will."

"And remember we're a team," Bella said, giving him a big hug and a kiss. She ran out the door before he could change his mind.

CHAPTER 28
The Audition

O n the day of the audition Bella stopped by Mary's on her way to Grandfather's.

"I'm so afraid he's going to back out," she said as Mary fixed her hair for her.

"Act confident," Mary said. "Think of how Lola would do it."

Bella smiled.

"What's so funny?"

"I met a cute young man at the radio station whom Lola would like very much," Bella said.

"She does like her men young," Mary chuckled.

"She likes them any age. I miss her so much."

"No one could make me laugh like her," Mary said.

"She's not gone forever," Bella said. "I'm not giving up until she's free."

"The trolley awaits us, Señor García," Bella called as she knocked on Grandfather's front door.

"I'm really too old for this." Grandfather didn't get up from his chair, but he looked elegant in his white suit coat and shirt, gold cuff links, silk tie, and dark pants.

"Today is your chance to prove that radio can have a higher and more honorable purpose," Bella said.

"So now it comes down to honor?" Grandfather gave Bella a wry smile.

"Indeed it does." Bella grinned. "Your hat, señor?" She took his hat from the stand and handed it to him.

Grandfather looked up at the shiny WTAM sign. "I know you meant well, but—"

"You'll be great." Bella snatched the door open and pulled him inside.

"May I help you?" the secretary asked.

"We have an appointment to see Mr. Parsons," Bella said.

The woman frowned at her appointment calendar. "I don't see anything. Are you sure?"

"I'm positive," Bella said.

"Miss Lorente," a voice interrupted. "You're right on time."

Bella looked up. Parsons was walking down the hall.

"You must be Mr. Lorente." He clapped his left hand on Grandfather's shoulder and shook his hand with his right.

"My name is Roberto García."

169

"Pleased to meet you. This little girl of yours is a knockout." Parsons winked at Bella. "Howard's in a meeting right now. If you folks'll have a seat, he should be finished shortly."

The springs of the couch squeaked as Grandfather and Bella sat down. "I feel like I'm waiting to have surgery," Grandfather whispered.

"They're going to love you," Bella said. "They will."

The secretary went back to her typing. Bella knew that Grandfather hated typewriters as much as he hated radios. "A letter should be written by hand," he often said. "How insulting and lazy to have a machine do your writing for you."

After the secretary had finished her letter and answered two phone calls, Grandfather pulled out his watch and frowned.

"I'm sure it won't be much longer," Bella said.

He shifted his hat from one hand to the other and looked at the door. "I'm sorry, Bella, but this wasn't meant to be."

"It wouldn't hurt to give a little notice when you set these things up, Jim." A voice drifted down the hall. Parsons and an older man were walking their way.

"Mr. García and Miss Lorente," Parsons said. "I'd like you to meet Robert Howard, our station manager."

"Nice of you to stop by." Howard extended his hand to Grandfather. "Jim tells me you're willing to try a reading."

Grandfather's legs were stiff as he got up. "I am pleased to meet you, Mr. Howard." Grandfather shook his hand.

"Call me Bob. If you'll come this way, the studio should be ready." Howard and Parsons started down the hall.

Grandfather turned to Bella. He looked old and tired.

His suit was rumpled, and his hair was plastered down on one side.

"Won't it be exciting if the radio turns out to be your new calling?" Bella said.

"The mike is waiting," Parsons called.

"You said you'd do it for me." Bella took Grandfather's hand. "And we've come all this way."

With a sigh, Grandfather turned to follow the men. Bella was feeling good until she saw the bright lights of the studio. Three of the walls were covered with floor-to-ceiling curtains, and the fourth held a glass-windowed control booth. A microphone stood at the front of the room. In the near corner a glamorous woman in a silky green dress was sitting at a piano bench and reading the lines of a script to a man.

"Testing." Parsons tapped on the microphone and spoke. "Testing oneski, twoski, threeski." Laughing, he turned to the sound engineer, who sat behind a panel of electric switches and dials.

"The level's fine," the engineer said.

"Let's start with this." Parsons handed Grandfather a typed page. "You go first, and then we'll try Miss Lorente."

Grandfather scanned the paper. "You want me to read this?"

"Since we're planning a Spanish story hour, we've worked up a little commercial," Parsons said.

"Selling soap?" Grandfather frowned.

"Give her a shot." Parsons patted Grandfather's shoulder.

Grandfather pulled a handkerchief from his vest pocket and dabbed his brow. He started reading the commercial, but

Parsons stopped him. "Could you hold the paper to one side? You're covering up the mike."

Grandfather moved the paper and leaned into the microphone. It made a loud squeal. "Whoa!" said Parsons. "That's a bit too close."

As Grandfather read the commercial, no one paid attention to him. Bella had never heard Grandfather's voice sound so weak and raspy. Parsons kept whispering to Mr. Howard, and the woman at the piano bench continued to rehearse her lines. Bella wished that Juan Fernandez were there to quiet everyone by ringing his bell as he did at the factory.

Grandfather coughed, and he looked very gray and pale.

Parsons looked up. "Everything okay, gramps?"

Before Grandfather could answer, Bella reached into her purse and pulled out a worn volume. She walked to Grandfather and put the book in his hand. Then she turned to Parsons. "Señor García would prefer to read from a novel."

"But we really need to see how the sponsor's material matches up with—"

"This will only take a moment." Bella stepped aside.

Grandfather looked Bella in the eye and nodded as he took his place in front of the microphone. "I will now read for you *The Delightful History of the Most Ingenious Knight, Don Quixote de La Mancha,* by Miguel de Cervantes."

When Mr. Howard heard the change in Grandfather's tone, he waved for Parsons to be quiet. The soundman looked up from behind the control panel, and the woman in green set down her script. Grandfather read in perfect Castilian Spanish:

"In a village of La Mancha, the name of which I do not wish

to recall, there lived a little while ago one of those gentlemen who are wont to keep a lance in the rack, an old buckler, a lean horse, and a swift greyhound. . . ."

Thus began the tale of Cervantes' gentle knight of La Mancha, a man who took it upon himself to right the wrongs of the world. Bella smiled as Grandfather continued. Though Quixote blundered through life, his heart was pure and his intentions were noble. And like Roberto García, through the most difficult of times, he remained a man of honor.

As Grandfather's deep, resonant voice continued, the woman at the piano bench stood up and quietly made her way to Bella's side. She leaned toward Bella and whispered, "Who is that man?"

"That is Roberto García, the finest *lector* in all of Ybor City," Bella said.

When Grandfather finished his reading, the staff stood in silence. Bella applauded, thinking of the loud clapping of *chavetas* that such a performance would have brought at El Paraíso.

Mr. Howard whispered something to Parsons; then he approached Grandfather. "That was a fine reading," he said. "I can't understand the lingo myself, but you just might fit the bill."

Parsons looked at Bella. "And I'm sure that Miss Lorente would be willing to handle the commercials."

"Certainly," Bella said.

Howard extended his hand to Grandfather. "So what do you say? Do we have a deal?"

"You'll have to speak with my manager." Grandfather winked at Bella.

CHAPTER 29
Hidalgo's Gesture

As Bella and Grandfather turned the corner by their *casita,* he whispered, "Look sad."

"But why?" Bella stopped when she saw Mary waiting on the front porch along with Mama and the children.

Grandfather walked slowly down the sidewalk, keeping his head down and shuffling his feet. He led Bella right past the Lorentes' until Juanita yelled, "Grandfather!"

He turned, pretending to be confused. Bella could see the worry in Mama's and Mary's faces.

"Did it go badly?" Mama asked.

Grandfather suddenly doffed his hat and turned to Bella. "Thanks to this young woman, I'm going to be an electric *lector.*"

"Hooray!" Juanita and Isabel ran and hugged Bella and Grandfather. "We owe a lot to Mary, too," Bella said, squeezing her friend around the shoulders.

"I'm so proud of you all," Mama said.

The following Saturday morning Bella was at Grandfather's house when someone knocked.

Bella walked to the front door. It was Cesar Hidalgo.

She was surprised when Grandfather extended his hand and said, "Welcome, Cesar. May I offer you a chair?"

"I can't stay. I only wanted to do a small favor out of appreciation for all your fine readings."

"You don't owe me anything."

"I've been saving up those quarters I refused to pay you."

"But I thought—"

"I admit I've cursed you for being Spanish in the past," Cesar said. "But I decided that twenty years is too long to hold a grudge. Besides, your work has given me much comfort."

"I was simply doing my job," Grandfather said.

"A job artfully done, señor," Cesar said. "But on to the business at hand. Since I have only myself to provide for, I decided to put all my quarters to good use before I left town."

"You're leaving Ybor?"

"I'm taking the train to Trenton, New Jersey, today. The union secretary told me about a factory up there that respects workers' rights. But if they don't treat me properly, I'll move elsewhere."

"I know you won't be afraid to speak your mind." Grandfather chuckled.

"The truth is important to me. As is honor. So if you would do me the honor of accepting a gift as payment on an account that is long overdue, please come this way." Cesar waved toward the front door.

"It's not like you to talk in riddles, Cesar." Grandfather shook his head as he stepped onto the porch.

Bella was ready to yell, "No! Don't trust him!"

But Grandfather shouted, "I don't believe it!" and ran down the steps.

Aunt Lola was walking up the sidewalk!

Lola gave Grandfather a big hug; then she turned and embraced Bella. "It's been a long time, dearie."

As Lola and Bella both wept, Grandfather turned to Cesar. "I don't understand. How could you have?"

Cesar grinned. "Ybor politicians will even listen to us Cubans if they see our wallets are fat enough."

Lola patted Cesar on the shoulder. "Can you believe it? Cesar bought them off," she said. "A guard came to my cell early this morning and said the judge wanted to see me. At first I thought they were going to rough me up. I said, 'I'm not going anywhere with you.'

"The guard got a funny look on his face and said, 'I'm not supposed to say anything, but I think you're getting out due to medical problems.' "

"Does your head still hurt?" Bella was worried.

Lola laughed. " 'Medical problems?' I told him, 'There's nothing wrong with this head other than a few loose screws.' " She tapped herself on the temple.

Cesar chuckled. "A doctor friend agreed to write a letter and help out."

Lola said, "The guard took me to the judge's chambers, and the judge said that due to my chronic pain, he was ordering me released with full credit for my time served. He said the only condition I had to follow was not to consort with any former or current members of the Tobacco Workers International Union.

"For a minute I thought about making a ruckus over what was clearly an under-the-table deal. Then I decided I could do a whole lot more for the other workers if I was free. Especially since the trial is due to start any day now."

"You agreed not to associate with the union?" Grandfather asked.

"I agreed not to 'consort.' " Lola winked. "But I have no idea what that means."

Cesar said, "She already stopped at the union office."

"Tía Lola!" Bella said.

"Nobody else in this town would ever hire me except the union," Lola said.

"The police will put you back in jail," Bella said.

"I don't think so, dearie." Lola winked again. "Not when I happen to know the name of a certain prominent judge who is clearly living off bribes."

"I must be catching my train," Cesar said.

Lola turned and hugged Cesar so hard that she knocked his hat from his hand. "I owe you a bunch."

"Perhaps you'd like to accompany me to New Jersey?" Cesar smoothed the ends of his mustache as he picked up his hat.

"I've seen the winters up north," Lola laughed.

"If you ever change your mind," Cesar said, "the union office in Trenton will know how to find me."

"I'll stop by if I'm ever in the neighborhood." Lola kissed his cheek before he turned to go. Then she threw her arms around Bella and Grandfather. "I plan to beat a drum on every street corner until we raise enough money to throw those crooks out of city hall."

Bella smiled. Though Lola's face was still thin and pale, her eyes had a hint of their old spark.

CHAPTER 30
El Lector of the Air

For the first *Spanish Story Hour* program, Grandfather performed the stories and Bella read the commericals. "Good afternoon, radio listeners." She began the show standing in front of the microphone while a background singer hummed. "Welcome to WTAM's *Spanish Story Hour,* brought to you by Super Suds, the miracle dishwashing soap that is guaranteed to protect the smooth, white loveliness of your hands."

When it was Grandfather's turn, Bella whispered, "Just think of this microphone as your new lectern."

Grandfather nodded. When he began, time stopped. "What a voice," someone whispered from the corner of the studio, as every person in the room turned and stared. At the end of the program even the janitor applauded.

Bella and Grandfather were still excited from the performance when they got off the trolley and walked up the street toward home. As they turned onto their block, Bella was startled by a shout. "Here they are!"

It was Tía Lola. Everyone from the neighborhood had gathered in front of the Navarros', and the moment they saw Grandfather and Bella, they applauded and cheered.

Juanita and Isabel ran up and hugged Grandfather. "We all listened to your program," Juanita said.

"You were wonderful," Isabel said.

"And so were you." Mama smiled at Bella.

"It's time to celebrate." Lola waved toward a table on the sidewalk that was heaped with food.

"Doesn't this remind you of the big Christmas party Mr. Ybor gave the workers in the old days, Grandfather?" Pedro said.

"It's even better!" Grandfather said.

When Bella brought her first paycheck home from the radio station, Mama said, "I can't believe how much our fortunes have changed. First Lola gets out of jail. Then this."

"They're paying me as much as the factory did," Bella said, "and I only have to work on Sunday."

"Best of all"—Mama hugged Bella—"you've helped the Lorentes earn back their dignity."

"And reading those commercials is a holiday compared to working in the stripping room," Bella said.

"It's also much better for the smooth, white loveliness of your hands!" Mama laughed.

Lola worked day and night at the union office. She wrote letters and made phone calls to raise money for a legal defense fund. It made no difference that the court threatened to charge the union with racketeering. "Can you imagine the nerve of them," she told Bella, "when they're the ones who've been taking *bolita* payoffs all these years?"

The first night when Mama invited Lola to dinner, Lola mainly talked about the workers who remained in jail. She never said a word about herself until Pedro asked, "Was it hard?"

"Was what hard, honey?" Lola asked.

"Jail," Pedro said.

"Let's just say there's nothing worse than losing your freedom. Imagine being locked in a cell half the size of your bedroom, with one tiny window, and not knowing if you're going to stay there ten days or ten years. And a bunch of stupid cracker guards—" Lola stopped when she saw Juanita's eyes fill up. "But my biggest problem was that I do not look good in prison stripes."

Juanita and Isabel both ran to the other side of the table and gave Lola a big hug. "Please don't ever go back there, Tía Lola," Isabel whispered.

Lola hugged both girls. "Don't worry your pretty heads."

"How's the new lawyer doing?" Grandfather asked.

"Instead of telling us what we want to hear like that first crook, he says we should expect to lose this trial because we have no chance of a fair hearing in Tampa. He knows the appeals court will be stacked against us too. But he's confident we'll get an honest ruling before the Florida Supreme Court."

For his third radio program Grandfather invited Bella to read de Maupassant's short story "The Necklace" with him. Though they'd practiced several times at home, Bella was nervous. Her role, that of the vain Mathilde Loisel, was the most important part in the story. Reading commercials had been simple, but she wanted to make Grandfather proud.

Grandfather introduced the story and began reading the part of Monsieur Loisel, a clerk who receives an invitation to a fancy government party. Thinking Mathilde will be happy, he hurries home with the news.

"And what do you suppose I am to wear to such an affair?" Bella leaned toward the microphone that stood between her and Grandfather, and she read in her harshest voice, tears trickling down her cheeks.

"Why, the dress you go to the theater in. It—it looks very nice to me." Grandfather stammered to show the clerk's confusion.

The talk between Grandfather and Bella went smoothly as the crafty Mathilde used her tears to secure a new dress and to borrow a diamond necklace from a friend.

Bella admired the way Grandfather countered Mathilde's anger with gentleness. After a lifetime of using his booming voice to fill the corners of a factory hall, he'd learned that the microphone could pick up the softest tones. With whispers Grandfather breathed life into the character of the sad clerk.

Toward the middle of the story Bella stumbled badly. Then she tried to make up for it by reading so fast that her words ran together. After all their practice!

But Grandfather smiled and spoke even more slowly than normal. "Take a breath, my dear." Grandfather touched her arm and pretended his speech was a part of their script. "Enjoy the special flavor of each word."

"So pace is the key to proper delivery, *monsieur*?" Bella asked with a smile, staying in character.

"Pace is the key in life as well, *mademoiselle*. For our silences speak as loudly as our words." Grandfather beamed.

The heart-wrenching conclusion of the story was met by applause from everyone in the studio. Grandfather bowed to Bella and said, "Superbly done."

As they walked to catch the trolley a short while later, Grandfather said, "The enemy has treated us well today."

"The enemy?" Bella asked.

"The radio," Grandfather laughed. "The machine I so hated has suddenly become our friend. You're doing wonderfully well. Next week I think we should try a more challenging work."

"Such as?"

"Our listeners might enjoy it if we continued our French theme with a reading from Hugo's *Les Misérables*. Would you be willing to play Cosette?"

"But of course, Monsieur Valjean."

Grandfather and Bella had just finished their first rehearsal of the Hugo reading when Lola stopped by with news of the cigar workers' case. "The decision finally came."

Bella could tell the news wasn't good.

"We lost on every count," Lola said. "Now we can only hope for the court to show mercy."

The sentence was a shock to all of Ybor. "They know how to kick us when we're down," Lola said.

"How bad was it?" Bella asked.

"The workers were sentenced to a total of fifty-three years." Lola shook her head. "Fifty-three years in prison for stepping into the street without a parade permit."

"You will file an appeal?" Grandfather asked.

"Yes, but how do we keep their hopes up in the meantime?"

"If anyone can lift their spirits, you can," Bella said.

Bella worried about Tía Lola. What if the police decided to make an example of her? Would her threat to turn in a crooked judge be enough to save her from a second trip to jail?

Despite these fears, in the weeks that followed, Bella enjoyed doing the female voices in classic scenes from *Don Quixote* (she played Dulcinea) and Zola's coal mining story, *Germinal* (Bella read the part of Catherine). One big surprise was the number of listeners who wrote letters to WTAM, praising *The Spanish Story Hour.* And residents of Ybor often stopped Grandfather and Bella on the street, saying, "Señor García," or "Señorita Lorente, it is an honor to see you. I so enjoy your program." Then they would mention their favorite reading from the previous week.

"This is a miracle," Grandfather said to Bella one afternoon. "In my largest factory I read to four hundred workers, but through the magic of radio we are reaching many more."

"There must be thousands of folks listening," Bella said.

Pedro nodded. "My friends say that when they walk down the street, every radio in the city is tuned to your show."

After Grandfather had gone home, Pedro smiled at Bella.

"What are you thinking?" Bella asked.

"Nothing," Pedro said, though his eyes glinted.

"Don't get into trouble," Bella said.

"Not anymore," Pedro said.

Bella didn't find out what Pedro had on his mind until the following week. The family had just finished Sunday dinner. Grandfather stood up and said, "Bella and I must be getting to the studio," and Pedro said, "I have a surprise for you first."

Pedro ran to the bedroom.

Grandfather looked at Bella for an explanation, but she could only shake her head.

Pedro returned with a sheet of paper and a cigar box. "What is this?" Grandfather asked as Pedro handed him a list of numbers and names. "Did you get a perfect score on a test?"

"Look closer." Pedro leaned over Grandfather's shoulder.

Bella glanced down. The names on the paper were all

residents of Ybor City and Tampa. Behind each name was the number 25. "There must be a hundred names on this paper," Grandfather said.

"A hundred and twenty-seven," Pedro said. "And see the last name?" he pointed to the bottom of the list.

"That's you." Grandfather looked confused.

"Which is why I'm giving you this." Pedro handed Grandfather a quarter. "And there are many more people waiting to sign up."

"I don't understand." Grandfather stared at the quarter Pedro had given him.

"The twenty-five behind each person's name means that they liked your radio show so much that they've paid you a quarter." Pedro flipped open the cigar box. "This is what I've collected in just one week." The box was heaped with coins.

"But why would people pay? The radio is free."

"Everyone wants it to be like the old days when you were their *lector*," Pedro said. "And they'd like a chance to vote on the authors you read." He showed Grandfather a second sheet of paper. "These are the names they've asked for so far."

"Pérez Galdós, Shakespeare, Molière, Valdés, Dickens," Grandfather read slowly. "All fine writers. But—"

"The people of Ybor would be honored if you would keep reading the classics for them," Pedro said.

Bella smiled at Pedro's cleverness in bringing up honor.

Grandfather sat down in a chair. "I'm overwhelmed." Julio climbed up into his lap and hugged him.

Bella patted Grandfather's arm. "Don't you always say 'What good is bread to a man if he cannot satisfy his hunger for the truth?'"

"You both use my own words against me," Grandfather said. "But if it's the will of the people I have no choice." He turned to Mama. "What do you think?"

"There's no one more qualified for the job," Mama said.

"Think of all the books you could buy with your money," Isabel said.

"That's true," Grandfather said. "And if Pedro's accounting can be trusted, there might be money left over for Bella's schooling."

"That's what I was hoping." Pedro stood proudly.

"I've also been considering a small present for your mother," Grandfather said.

"I have everything I need," Mama said.

"I saw an ad in the paper the other day for a contraption called an Easy Washer," Grandfather said.

"A washing machine!" Mama said.

"Complete with a porcelain tub and a rust-resistant wringer." Grandfather smiled.

"After all the years you've rubbed your knuckles bare on a scrub board, you deserve it," Bella said.

"And"—Lola looked at Grandfather—"your program might be able to contribute to the cigar workers' defense fund."

"*The Spanish Story Hour* will also show the cigar companies that tearing out lecterns in the dark of the night will not silence Roberto García!" Bella said.

Pedro said, "And I can pass out flyers advertising you as *El Lector* of the Air."

"Let's remember our dignity," Grandfather said.

"Yes. We have our professional reputations to consider." Bella laughed and hugged Grandfather's arm.

CHAPTER 31
El Paraíso Revisited

The *Spanish Story Hour* soon had more than three hundred subscribers. While Pedro picked up the money, Bella and Mary kept track of the contributions and the reading requests. Most people didn't ask Grandfather to read a certain story but said, "Tell *El Lector* to read whatever he chooses."

One woman sent a letter along with her quarter: "It is not so much what Señor García reads as how he reads it. That man could turn the weather report into a symphony if he set his mind to it. Such music!" Mary's father even heard about *The Spanish Story Hour* out in Colorado, and he sent a postcard to congratulate Grandfather and Bella. He also told Bella that he planned to surprise Mary with a visit that spring.

As the program's popularity grew, Grandfather insisted on paying Bella and Mary a salary for answering letters and doing the bookkeeping. One day as Bella was opening an envelope, she told Mary, "If we keep saving our money there'll be no reason why we can't start high school in the fall. And I can stay on the radio, since we broadcast on Sunday."

"I suppose," Mary said.

"You don't sound very excited."

"I've been thinking I might want to go to beauty school."

"And be a hairdresser?"

"I know we've always planned on going to high school together," Mary said, "but I think it would be fun to make women beautiful."

At first, Bella was disappointed, but after she had thought for a while, she said, "Well, you're much better at fixing hair than anyone I know—even Lola. So I guess our dreams don't have to be the same. As long as I know you'll always be my best friend."

Fan letters for *The Spanish Story Hour* kept arriving from all over Florida and South Carolina and Georgia. "How can these people have heard my program?" Grandfather asked.

"Once the sun goes down," Pedro said, "radio waves can travel hundreds of miles."

Bella held out the letters. "Two came from New York and one each from Chicago and Cleveland."

"Amazing," Grandfather said.

"Who knows?" Bella said. "When conditions are right your voice may travel all the way to Spain."

"Spain?" Grandfather shook his head.

"Radio waves fly that far in seconds," Pedro said.

"And to think of the many days it took my family to steam across the ocean when I was a boy."

"The *presidente* of the new Spanish republic may hear you on the radio some evening!" Pedro said.

On her way to Cannella's market the next day, Bella walked past a place she had long been avoiding. She stopped in front of El Paraíso. Now that the paradise tree was gone, the weathered wooden building looked shabby in the unshaded light. Radio music blared from the second-story window. Bella could hear the clank of cigar-rolling machines inside. The only thing that hadn't changed was the blue haze of cigar smoke that drifted out the windows.

She walked across the lawn to the place where the yellow-flowered tree had stood. She took a deep breath. The smell of moist tobacco mingled with the scent of broken seashells and earth that rose from foundation trenches workmen had been digging in the lawn. Bella missed the delicate scent of paradise tree blossoms. By summer a new addition to the factory would house more cigar-rolling machines. Perhaps Grandfather's prediction would soon come true and El Paraíso would be one long row of machines empty of people.

Bella turned to the north and saw only empty sky where the broad crown of the tree had been. A crooked stump, its top puddled with sap, burned under the spring sun. And a fat bee buzzed over the clumps of dried purple berries that had been trampled into the grass.

Just then the shadow of a bird flicked across the lawn. Bella looked up and saw the white wing patch and tail of a mockingbird as it flapped over the factory roof. Where would the birds nest now that the tree had been cut down?

Before Bella started back toward the sidewalk, she glanced down and saw that a spindly seedling had sprouted in the shadow of the stump. She touched the pink-veined leaf of a tiny paradise tree.

Bella smiled. Like Don Quixote, the paradise tree refused to surrender. As Bella started toward home, the trolley bell clanged downtown, and the faint scent of mudflats and mangroves blew in from Hillsborough Bay. The freshening wind meant that children's voices would soon be chasing kite tails across the sky.

AFTERWORD

Fifteen cigar workers were arrested in front of Ybor City's Labor Temple on November 7, 1931, and charged with "unlawful assembly, rioting, and assault to commit murder." The thirteen men and two women were convicted in January 1932, and on February 1 they were sentenced to a total of fifty-three years in prison. When the union attempted to raise money for a defense fund, the court charged it with racketeering.

The Florida Supreme Court overturned the convictions in May 1933, ruling that the police had violated the law by not ordering the crowd to disperse before they arrested the workers. All the defendants were freed.

ACKNOWLEDGMENTS

A number of former residents of Ybor City and scholars of Florida history were generous in helping me with this novel. Primary among them were Willie Garcia, attorney-at-law; Robert Ingalls, PhD; Robert Arsenau, PhD; Gary Mormino, PhD; Sonia Cruz; Sam Ficarrotta; Yael Greenburg; Arsineo Sanchez; Ferdie Pacheco, MD; Patrick Manteiga, Editor of *La Gaceta;* Paul Camp, University of South Florida Library, Special Collections; Jeneice Sorrentino and the staff of the Ybor City Campus Library; Kathleen Winter, *Tampa Tribune* archivist; Kathleen Barber of the Florida State University Film School; and the staff and volunteers of the Ybor City Museum, including Javier Puig, Maureen Patrick, Helen Ficari, and Pam Bushman. And special thanks to Erik Read for sharing his Tornado Soup idea.

Here are some other books from Pineapple Press on related topics. For a complete catalog, visit our website at www.pineapplepress.com. Or write to Pineapple Press, P.O. Box 3889, Sarasota, Florida 34230-3889, or call (800) 746-3275.

Fiction

A Land Remembered, Student Edition by Patrick Smith. The sweeping story of three generations of MacIveys, who work their way up from a dirt-poor Cracker life to the wealth and standing of real estate tycoons. Volume 1 covers the first generation of MacIveys to arrive in Florida and Zech's coming of age. Volume 2 covers Zech's son, Solomon, and the exploitation of the land as his own generation prospers. Age 9 and up.

Blood Moon Rider by Zack C. Waters. When his Marine father is killed in WWII, young Harley Wallace is exiled to the Florida cattle ranch of his grandfather. The murder of a cowman and the disappearance of Grandfather Wallace lead Harley and his new friend Beth on a wild ride through the swamps and into the midst of a conspiracy of evil. Ages 9–14.

Escape to the Everglades by Edwina Raffa and Annelle Rigsby. Based on historical fact, this young adult novel tells the story of Will Cypress, a half-Seminole boy living among his mother's people during the Second Seminole War. He meets Chief Osceola and travels with him to St. Augustine. Ages 9–14.

Solomon by Marilyn Bishop Shaw. Eleven-year-old Solomon Freeman and his parents, Moses and Lela, survive the Civil War, gain their freedom, and gamble their dreams, risking their very existence on a homestead in the remote environs of north central Florida. Ages 9–14.

Kidnapped in Key West by Edwina Raffa and Annelle Rigsby. Twelve-year-old Eddie Malone is living in the Florida Keys in 1912 when suddenly his world is turned upside down. His father, a worker on Henry Flagler's Over-Sea Railroad, is thrown into jail for stealing the railroad payroll. Eddie is determined to prove his father's innocence. But then the real thieves kidnap Eddie. Can he escape? Will he ever get home? Will he be able to prove Pa's innocence? Ages 8–12.

The Treasure of Amelia Island by M.C. Finotti. These are the ruminations of Mary Kingsley, the youngest child of former slave Ana Jai Kingsley, as she recounts the life-changing events of December 1813. Her family lives in *La Florida,* a Spanish territory under siege by patriots who see no place for freed people of color in a new Florida. Against these mighty events, Mary decides to search for a legendary pirate treasure with her brothers. Ages 8–12.

Esmeralda and the Enchanted Pond by Susan Jane Ryan. Esmeralda visits a mysterious pond with her dad. While she wants real, scientific explanations for the natural phenomena all around her, her dad offers imaginary, mystical answers. Much to her delight, he finally reveals the science behind the enchanted pond. Ages 8–11.

The Old Man and the C by Carole Tremblay. Meet Charlie, whose dream is to catch the biggest fish in the sea. He signs up for a fishing tournament, but what he catches is a big surprise. Unlike Hemingway's hero, Charlie turns his quest for a big fish into an amusing adventure that involves a bad case of the hiccups. Ages 6–10.

Nonfiction

Those Amazing Animals series. Written by various authors, each book in the series offers 20 questions and answers sure to engage children and teach them about animals such as alligators, owls, turtles, eagles, pelicans, butterflies, manatees, dolphins, flamingos, vultures, and lizards. Lots of color pictures and funny illustrations. Ages 5–9.

America's REAL First Thanksgiving by Robyn Gioia. When most Americans think of the first Thanksgiving, they think of the Pilgrims and the Indians in New England in 1621. But on September 8, 1565, the Spanish and the native Timucua celebrated with a feast of Thanksgiving in St. Augustine. Teacher's activity guide also available. Ages 9–14.

The Young Naturalist's Guide to Florida, Second Edition by Peggy Sias Lantz and Wendy A. Hale. Provides up-to-date information about Florida's wonderful natural places and the plants and creatures that live here, many of which are found nowhere else in the United States. Learn about careers in the environmental field and how to help protect Florida's beautiful places. Ages 10–14.

Florida Lighthouses for Kids by Elinor De Wire. Learn why some lighthouses are tall and some are short, why a cat parachuted off St. Augustine Lighthouse, and much more. Lots of color pictures. Age 9 and up.

Native Americans in Florida by Kevin M. McCarthy. Long before the first European explorers set foot on Florida soil, numerous Native American tribes hunted, honored their gods, and built burial mounds. This book explores the importance of preserving the past and how archaeologists do their work. The different types of Indian mounds and their uses are explained, as well as Indian languages and reservations. Age 10 and up.

African Americans in Florida by Maxine D. Jones and Kevin McCarthy. Profiles more than fifty African Americans during four centuries of Florida history in brief essays. Traces the role African Americans played in the discovery, exploration, and settlement of Florida as well as through the Civil War to the Civil Rights movement. Age 10 and up.

Legends of the Seminoles by Betty Mae Jumper with Peter Gallagher. For the first time, stories and legends handed down through generations by tribal elders have been set down for all to enjoy. Each tale is illustrated with an original color painting. All ages.

Hunted Like a Wolf: The Story of the Seminole War by Milton Meltzer. Award winning young adult book that offers a look at the events, players, and political motives leading to the Second Seminole War. It explores the Seminoles' choices and sacrifices and the treachery of the U.S. during that harsh time. Age 12 and up.

Iguana Invasion!: Exotic Pets Gone Wild in Florida by Virginia Aronson and Ally Szejko. Green iguanas, Burmese pythons, Nile monitor lizards, rhesus monkeys, and many more kinds of nonnative animals are rapidly increasing their populations in subtropical Florida. This full-color book provides scientific information, exciting wildlife stories, and identification photos for the most common exotic animals on the loose, most of them the offspring of abandoned pets. Age 12 and up.

The Gopher Tortoise: A Life History by Patricia Ashton and Ray Ashton Jr. Color photos and simple text illustrate the behavior and daily life of this endangered animal. Explains the critical role this tortoise and its burrow play in the upland ecosystem of Florida and the Southeast. Learn how scientists study them and try to protect them. Age 10 and up.

Marjory Stoneman Douglas and the Florida Everglades by Sandra Wallus Sammons. Read about the "grandmother of the Everglades," from her childhood up North to her long and inspiring life in south Florida. She won the Presidential Medal of Freedom for her work. Ages 9–12.

Marjorie Kinnan Rawlings and the Florida Crackers by Sandra Wallus Sammons. Marjorie Kinnan Rawlings always loved to write. When she moved to Cross Creek in Florida, she began to write stories about the Crackers she met. *The Yearling,* about a boy and his pet deer, won a Pulitzer Prize for fiction. Ages 9–12.

The Two Henrys: Henry Plant and Henry Flagler and Their Railroads by Sandra Wallus Sammons. Henry Plant and Henry Flagler changed the landscape of Florida in the late 1800s and early 1900s. This dual biography is the story of railroads and the men whose innovation and money built them. Flagler opened up the east coast of Florida with his railroads and hotels, and Plant did the same on the west coast. Age 12 and up.

Henry Flagler, Builder of Florida by Sandra Wallus Sammons. Henry Morrison Flagler was already a millionaire when he first visited Florida in 1878. He came back and built railroads along the east coast of the state so others could more easily travel there. Then he built grand hotels so those travelers had a place to stay. By 1912 he had built a railroad all the way to Key West. Determined and practical, Flagler met all the great challenges he set for himself. Ages 9–12.

Konnichiwa Florida Moon by Virginia Aronson. This is the story of George Morikami, a poor Japanese immigrant who became a millionaire in south Florida. He made his fortune from the land by growing pineapples and buying more land. The beautiful garden he created still exists as the Morikami Museum and Japanese Gardens in Delray Beach. Ages 8–12.

Gift of the Unicorn by Virginia Aronson. Lue Gim Gong came to Florida as a boy from his native China. He overcame poverty and discrimination to become a brilliant horticulturist who developed world-famous citrus species. Ages 10–14.

Old Florida Style: A Story of Cracker Cattle (DVD) by Steve Kidd and Alex Menendez (Delve Productions, Inc.). Saddle up a Cracker horse called a marsh tacky and explore old Florida, when cow hunters pulled the tough little Spanish cattle out of the palmettos and established this as a cattle state. This DVD showcases Florida's Cracker heritage. All ages.

Patchwork: Seminole and Miccosukee Art and Activities by Dorothy Downs. Discover the history of the Seminole and Miccosukee people and how they do their crafts. Learn how to make your very own patchwork pattern and doll. Ages 9–12.

CPSIA information can be obtained
at www.ICGtesting.com
Printed in the USA
BVOW04s1638170317
478657BV00001B/1/P